Quinn's blue eyes locked [...] **that stirred an unexpected heat in her belly.**

Even when she knew with 100 percent certainty it was all an act.

She licked her lips, her mouth gone suddenly dry. She should say something. Prevent this farce that no one would ever believe. But then again...hadn't she promised herself she would make this a performance worth watching?

A show of passion?

"Now." His gaze never left hers even as he continued to address the media. "I am going to ask you to check Ms. Koslov's schedule for a new interview time tomorrow. Because tonight we have something private and wonderful to celebrate."

The camerawoman gave a quiet squeal of excitement. A few people clapped halfheartedly. Sofia wondered how she'd ever dared to ask Quinn McNeill for a temporary fiancé. She couldn't believe he'd granted her wish.

And not with his brother. But with Quinn himself as her fake groom.

The cameras captured every moment of this absurd dance as she clutched a bouquet in one hand while Quinn tucked the mysterious black velvet box into the other. Then, leaving no doubt as to his meaning, he slanted his lips over hers and kissed her.

* * *

The Magnate's Mail-Order Bride is part of the McNeill Magnates trilogy: Those McNeill men just have a way with women!

Dear Reader,

It's been a long time since I lived in Manhattan, but I'll never forget the energy of the city or the sense of being surrounded by people striving to achieve their dreams. New York represents the highest level of excellence in so many fields—from high finance to fashion and art.

Ballerina Sofia Koslov is one of those ambitious few who find a niche in this competitive city. As a principal dancer in one of the world's premiere companies, she has a lot to lose if she doesn't stay focused. But when a playboy billionaire proposes marriage in front of the media, she can't help but be distracted. Enter the billionaire's brother—equally wealthy but far more practical Quinn McNeill. Quinn offers a cover story for the media and whisks her out of the public eye.

Now Sofia can prepare for her next audition. Except she can't get Quinn off her mind. Especially when his suggestion for a fake engagement puts her in his compelling company far too often. It's the most exciting engagement of her life until Sofia discovers the real reason that all the McNeill magnates want to wed!

I hope you'll join me for more books in my new series, starting next month with *The Magnate's Marriage Merger*.

Happy reading!

Joanne Rock

JOANNE ROCK

THE MAGNATE'S
MAIL-ORDER BRIDE

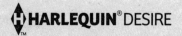

Recycling programs
for this product may
not exist in your area.

ISBN-13: 978-0-373-83840-0

The Magnate's Mail-Order Bride

Copyright © 2017 by Joanne Rock

Printed in U.S.A.

www.Harlequin.com

Four-time RITA® Award nominee **Joanne Rock** has penned over seventy stories for Harlequin. An optimist by nature and a perpetual seeker of silver linings, Joanne finds romance fits her life outlook perfectly—love is worth fighting for. A former Golden Heart® Award recipient, she has won numerous awards for her stories. Learn more about Joanne's imaginative Muse by visiting her website, joannerock.com, or following @joannerock6 on Twitter.

Books by Joanne Rock

Harlequin Superromance

Heartache, TN

Promises Under the Peach Tree
Nights Under the Tennessee Stars
Dances Under the Harvest Moon
Whispers Under a Southern Sky

Harlequin Desire

Bayou Billionaires

His Secretary's Surprise Fiancé
Secret Baby Scandal

The McNeill Magnates

The Magnate's Mail-Order Bride

Visit the Author Profile page at Harlequin.com, or joannerock.com, for more titles.

To Maureen Wallace, the empathetic
and efficient property manager on-site at the
vacation rental where I finished this book.
When construction work outside my rental
made writing impossible, Maureen listened
to my tale of woe and found another spot for me,
making sure I could get work done the next day
and have a gorgeous water view to boot!
Thank you for going above and beyond to help.

One

"It's no wonder her performances lack passion. Have you ever seen Sofia date anyone in all the time we've known her?"

Normally, Sofia Koslov didn't eavesdrop. Yet hearing the whispered gossip stopped her in her tracks as she headed from the Gulfstream's kitchen back to her seat for landing.

A principal dancer in the New York City Ballet, Sofia had performed a brief engagement with a small dance ensemble in Kiev last week. Her colleagues had been all too glad to join her when her wealthy father had offered his private plane for their return to the United States. But apparently the favor hadn't won her any new allies. As one of the most rapidly promoted female dancers currently in the company, Sofia's successes had ruffled feathers along the way.

She clutched her worn copy of *A Midsummer Night's Dream* to her chest and peered toward her father's seat at the front of the jet, grateful he was still engrossed in a business teleconference call. Vitaly Koslov had accompanied the troupe on the trip to the Ukraine, his birthplace. He'd used their rare time together as an opportunity to pressure Sofia about settling down and providing him with grandchildren who might be more interested in taking over his global empire than she'd been.

"That's not fair, Antonia," one of the other dancers in the circle of four recliners snapped, not bothering to lower her voice. "None of us has time to meet people during the season. I haven't had a lover all year. Does that make me passionless when I go on stage?"

Sofia told herself she should walk back to her seat before the pilot told them to buckle up. But her feet stayed glued to the floor. She peered down at her notes on Shakespeare's play, pretending to reread them for an upcoming role as Titania if anyone happened to notice her.

"But Sofia's been with the company since ballet school and have we ever heard her name connected romantically with anyone?" Antonia Blakely had entered ballet school at the same time as Sofia, and had advanced to each level with the company faster than her. "Actually, her dad must agree that she's turning into a dried-up old prune, because—*get this*." She paused theatrically, having relied on showmanship over technical skill her entire career. Now, she lowered her voice even more. "I overheard her father talking to the *matchmaker* he hired for her."

Sofia's stomach dropped even though the plane hadn't started its descent. She gripped the wooden door frame that separated the kitchen from the seating area. For over a year she'd resisted her father's efforts to hire a matchmaking service on her behalf. But it was true—he'd stepped up the pressure during their visit to Ukraine, insisting she think about her family and her roots.

Marriage wasn't even on her radar while her career was on the upswing. Would Dad have signed her up with his matchmaker friend without her approval? Her gaze flicked back to the proud billionaire who made a fortune by trusting his gut and never doubting himself for a second.

Of course he would proceed without her agreement. Betrayal slammed through her harder than an off-kilter landing.

"Seriously?" one of the other dancers asked. "Like a private matchmaker?"

"Of course. Rich people don't use the same dating web sites as the rest of us. They try to find their own kind." Antonia spoke with that irritating assurance shared by know-it-alls everywhere. "If Papa Koslov gets his way, there'll be a rich boy ready and waiting for his precious daughter at the airport when we land."

Sofia lifted a hand to her lips to hold back a gasp and a handful of curses. She wasn't wealthy, for one thing. Her father might be one of the richest people in the world, but that didn't mean she was, too. She had never even spent a night under his roof until after her mother's death when Sofia was just thirteen. She'd followed her mother's example in dealing with him, drawing that financial line and refusing his support a long time ago. Her father equated money with power, and she wouldn't let him dictate her life. Ballet was her defiance—her choice of art over the almighty dollar.

Her father knew he couldn't control her choices. Not even Vitaly Koslov in all his arrogance would arrange for her to meet a prospective date in front of twenty colleagues. Not after an exhausting overseas dance schedule and nine hours in the air across seven time zones. Would he?

A ringing noise distracted her from the question and she peered around, only to realize the chime came from her pocket. Her cell phone. She must not have shut it off for the plane ride. Withdrawing the device, she muted the volume, but not before half the dancers on the plane turned to stare. Including the group nearby who'd been gossiping about her.

None of them looked particularly shamefaced.

Sofia hurried toward an open seat and buckled into the wide leather chair for descent. She checked the incoming text on her phone while the pilot made the usual announcements about the landing.

Her closest friend, Jasmine Jackson, worked in public relations and had agreed to help Sofia with a PR initiative this year to take her dance career to the next level. Jasmine's text was about the interview Sofia had agreed to for *Dance* magazine.

Reporter and one camera operator for Dance will meet you in terminal to film arrival. We want you to look like you're coming off a successful world tour! Touch up your makeup and no yoga pants, please.

Panic crawled up her throat at the idea of meeting with the media now when she was exhausted and agitated about the other dancers' comments. Still, she pulled out her travel duffel and fished around the bottom for her makeup bag to comply with Jasmine's wise advice. Chances were good that Antonia had misinterpreted her father's conversation anyhow. He might be high-handed and overbearing, but he'd known about the *Dance* magazine interview. She'd told him there was a chance the reporter would want to meet her at the airport. He wouldn't purposely embarrass her.

Unless he fully intended to put her on the spot? Prevent her from arguing with him by springing a new man on her while the cameras rolled?

Impossible. She shook off the idea as too over the top, even for him. She already had the lip gloss wand out when her phone chimed with another message from Jasmine.

WARNING—the camera person freelances for the tabloids. I'm not worried about you, of course, but maybe warn the other dancers? Good luck!

The plane wheels hit the tarmac with a jarring thud, nearly knocking the phone from her hand. Capping the lip gloss, she knew no amount of makeup was going to cover up the impending disaster. If Antonia was correct about her father's plans and some tabloid reporter captured the resulting argument between Sofia and her dad—the timing would be terrible. It would undermine everything she'd worked for in hiring a publicist in the first place.

Celebrated choreographer Idris Fortier was in town this week and he planned to create a ballet to premiere in New York. Sofia would audition for a feature role—as would every other woman on the plane. Competition could turn vicious at the slightest opportunity.

Maybe it already had.

Steeling herself for whatever happened in the terminal, Sofia took deep breaths to slow her racing heart. Forewarned was forearmed, right? She should consider herself fortunate that her gossipy colleague had given her a heads-up on her father's plan. With cameras rolling for her interview, she couldn't afford the slightest misstep. She could argue with him later, privately. But she wouldn't sacrifice a good PR opportunity when she had the chance of a lifetime to be the featured dancer in a new Idris Fortier ballet.

She would think of this as a performance and she would nail it, no matter what surprises the public stage had to offer. That's what she did, damn it.

And this time, no one would say her performance lacked passion.

* * *

"Don't do something stupid because you're angry." Quinn McNeill tried to reason with his youngest brother as he strode beside him toward the terminal of the largest private airport servicing Manhattan. They'd shared a limo to Teterboro from the McNeill Resorts' offices in midtown this afternoon even though Quinn's flight to Eastern Europe to meet with potential investors didn't leave for several hours. He'd canceled his afternoon meetings just to talk sense into Cameron.

"I'm not angry." Cameron spread his arms wide, his herringbone pea coat swinging open as if to say he had nothing to hide. "Look at me. Do I look upset?"

With his forced grin, actually, yes. The men shared a family resemblance, their Scots roots showing in blue eyes and dark hair. But when Quinn said nothing, Cameron continued, "I'm going to allow Gramps to dictate my life and move me around like a chess piece so that I can one day inherit a share of the family business. Which I don't really want in the first place except that he's drilled loyalty into our heads and he doesn't want anyone but a McNeill running McNeill Resorts."

Last week, Quinn, Cameron and their other brother, Ian, had all been called into their grandfather's lawyer's office for a meeting that spelled out terms of a revised will that would split the shares of the older man's global corporation into equal thirds among them. The news itself was no surprise since the McNeill patriarch had promised as much for years, grooming them for roles in his company even though each of them had gone on to develop their own business interests. Malcolm McNeill's apathetic only son had taken a brief turn at the company helm and proven himself unequal to the task, so the older man had targeted the next generation to inherit.

None of them *needed* the promised inheritance. But Cam was the closest to their grandfather and felt the most pressure to buy into Malcolm McNeill's vision for the future. And the catch was, each of them could only obtain his share of McNeill Resorts upon marriage, with the share reverting to the estate if the marriage ended sooner than twelve months.

Out of overinflated loyalty, Cameron seemed ready to tie the knot with a woman, sight-unseen, after choosing her from a matchmaker's lineup of foreign women eager to wed. Either that, or he was hoping a ludicrous trip to the altar would make their grandfather realize what a bad idea this was and prompt him to call the whole thing off.

It had always been tough to tell with Cam. For Quinn's part, he was content to take a wait-and-see approach and hope their grandfather changed his mind. The old man was still in good health. And he'd conveniently booked a trip to China after the meeting in his lawyer's office, making it next to impossible to argue with him for at least a few more weeks.

"Cam, look at it this way. If it's so important to Gramps that the company remain in family hands, he wouldn't have attached this new stipulation." Quinn ignored the phone vibrating in his pocket as he tried to convince his brother of the point.

"Gramps won't live forever." Cameron raised his voice as a jet took off overhead. "That will might be ludicrous, but it's still a legal document. I don't want the company to end up on the auction block for some investor to swoop in and divvy up the assets."

"Neither do I." Quinn's coattails flapped in the gust of air from the nearby takeoff. "But I'd rather try to convince the stubborn old man that forcing marriage down our throats might backfire and create more instability in the company than anything."

"Who says my marriage won't be stable? I might be on to something, letting a matchmaker choose my bride. It's not like I've had any luck finding Ms. Right on my own."

Cameron had a reputation as a playboy, a cheerful charmer who wined and dined some of the world's most beautiful women.

Quinn shook his head. "Since when have you tried looking for meaningful relationships?"

"I don't want someone who is playing an angle." Cameron scowled. "I meet too many women more interested in seeing what I can do for them."

"This girl could be doing the same thing. Maybe you're her ticket to permanent residence in the United States." Shouldering his way through a small group of businessmen who emerged from the terminal building stumbling and laughing, Quinn opened the door and held it for his brother. "How much do you know about your bride? You've never even spoken to this woman. Does she even speak English?"

Where the hell was their master negotiator brother, Ian, for conversations like this? Quinn needed backup and the reasonable voice of the middle son who had always mediated the vastly different perspectives Cameron and Quinn held. But Ian was in meetings all day, leaving Quinn to talk his brother out of his modern-day, mail-order bride scheme.

All around him, the airport seethed with activity as flights landed and drivers rushed in to handle baggage for people who never paused in their cell phone conversations.

Cameron led them toward the customs area where international flights checked in at one of two counters.

"I know her name is Sofia and that she's Ukrainian. Her file said she was marriage-minded, just like me." Cam pulled out his phone and flashed the screen under Quinn's nose. "That's her."

A picture of a beautiful woman filled the screen, her features reflecting the Eastern European ideal with high cheekbones and arched eyebrows that gave her a vaguely haughty look. With her bare shoulders and a wealth of beaded necklaces, however, the photo of the gray-eyed blonde bombshell had a distinctly professional quality.

Quinn felt as if he'd seen her somewhere before. A professional model, maybe?

"This is probably just a photo taken from a foreign

magazine and passed off as her. Photography like that isn't cheap. And did you pay for a private flight for this woman to come over here?" Not that it was his business how his brother spent his money. But damn.

Even for Cameron, that seemed excessive.

"Hell, no. She arranged her own flight. Or maybe the matchmaker did." He shrugged as though it didn't matter, but he'd obviously given this whole idea zero thought. Or thought about it only when he was angry with their grandfather. "Plus she's *Ukrainian*." He stressed the word for emphasis. "I figured she might be a help once you secure the Eastern European properties. Always nice to have someone close who speaks the language, and maybe Gramps will put me in charge of revamping the hotels once I've passed the marriage test." He said this with a perfectly straight face.

He had to be joking. Any second now Cameron would say "to hell with this" and walk out. Or laugh and walk out. But he wasn't going to greet some foreigner fresh off an international flight and propose.

Not even Cameron would go that far. Quinn put a hand on his brother's chest, halting him for a second.

"Do not try to pass off this harebrained idea as practical in any way." They shared a level gaze for a moment until Cameron pushed past, his focus on something outside on the tarmac.

Quinn's gaze went toward a handful of travelers disembarking near the customs counter. One of the women seemed to have caught her scarf around the handrail of the air stairs.

"That might be her now." Cameron's eyes were on the woman, as well. "I wish I'd brought some flowers." Pivoting, he jogged over to a counter decorated with a vase full of exotic blooms near the pilots' club.

Vaguely, Quinn noticed Cameron charming the attendant into selling him a few of the purple orchids. But Quinn's attention lingered on the woman who had just freed her pink printed scarf from the handrail. Although huge sunglasses covered half her face, with her blond hair and full, pouty lips, she resembled the woman in the photo. About twenty other people got off that same plane, a disproportionately high number of them young women.

Concern for his brother made him wary. The woman's closest travel companion appeared to be a slick-looking guy old enough to be her father. The man held out a hand to help her descend the steps. She was waif-thin and something about the way she carried herself seemed very deliberate. Like she was a woman used to being the center of attention. Quinn was missing something here.

"She's tiny." Cameron had returned to Quinn's side. "I didn't think to ask how tall she was."

Quinn's brain worked fast as he tried to refit the pieces that didn't add up. And to do it before the future Mrs. McNeill made it past the customs agent.

The other women in front of her sped through the declarations process.

"So who is supposed to introduce the two of you?" Quinn's bad feeling increased by the second. "Your

matchmaker set up a formal introduction, I hope?"
He should be going over his notes for his own meeting overseas tonight, not worrying about who would
introduce his foolish brother to a con artist waiting
to play him.

But how many times had Cameron stirred up trouble with one impulsive decision or another then simply walked away when things got out of hand, leaving
someone else to take care of damage control?

"No one." Cameron shrugged. "She just texted me
what time to meet the plane." He wiped nonexistent
lint off his collar and rearranged the flowers, a glint
of grim determination in his eyes.

"Cam, don't do this." Quinn didn't understand rash
people. How could he logically argue against this proposal when no logic had gone into his brother's decision in the first place? "At least figure out who she
really is before you drag her to the nearest justice of
the peace." They both watched as the woman tugged
off her sunglasses to speak with the customs agent,
her older travel companion still hovering protectively
behind her.

"Sofia's photo was real enough, though. She's a
knockout." Cameron's assessment sounded as dis-
passionate and detached as if he'd been admiring a
painting for one of the new hotels.

Quinn, on the other hand, found it difficult to remain impassive about the woman. There was something striking about her. She had a quiet, delicate
beauty and a self-assured air in her perfect posture

and graceful walk. And to compound his frustrations with his brother, Quinn realized what he was feeling for Cameron's future bride was blatant and undeniable physical attraction.

Cameron clapped a hand on his shoulder and moved toward the gate. "Admit it, Sofia is exactly as advertised."

Before Quinn could argue, a pair of women approached the doors leading outside. They were clearly waiting for someone. Both wore badges that dangled from ribbons around their necks, and one hoisted a professional-looking camera.

Reporters?

Cameron held the door for them and followed them out.

And like a train wreck that Quinn couldn't look away from, he watched as Cameron greeted the slender Ukrainian woman with a bouquet of flowers and—curse his eyes—a velvet box. He'd brought a *ring*? With his customary charm, Cameron bowed and passed Sofia the bouquet. Just in time for the woman with the camera to fix her lens on the tableaux.

Quinn rushed toward the scene—wanting to stop it and knowing it was too late. Had Cameron called a friend from the media? Had he wanted this thing filmed to be sure their grandfather heard about it? Whatever mess Cam was creating for himself, Quinn had the sinking feeling he'd be the one to dig him out of it.

Cold, dry, winter wind swept in through the door

and blasted him in the face at the same time Cameron's words hit his ears.

"Sofia, I've been waiting all day to meet my bride."

Two

Sofia had mentally prepared to be approached by a suitor. She had not expected a marriage proposal.

In all the years she'd danced Balanchine on toes that bled right through the calluses, all the times she'd churned out bravura fouetté turns fearing she'd fall in front of a live audience, she'd never been so disoriented as she was staring up at the tall, dark-haired man bearing flowers and…a ring?

The way she chose to handle this encounter would surely be recorded for posterity and nitpicked by those who would love nothing more than to see her make a misstep offstage. Or lose a chance at the lead in Fortier's first new ballet in two years.

In the strained silence, the wind blew Sofia's scarf off her shoulders to smother half her face. She could hear Antonia whispering behind her back. And giggling.

"For pity's sake, man, let's take this inside." Sofia's father was the first to speak.

Vitaly Koslov maintained his outward composure, but Sofia knew him well enough to hear the surprise in his tone. Was it possible he hadn't foreseen such a rash action from a suitor when he arranged for a matchmaker for her without her consent? The more she thought about it, the more she fumed. How dare this man corner her with his marriage offer in a public place?

She stepped out of the wind into the bright lobby, wishing she could just keep on walking out the front exit. But the camerawoman still trailed her. Sofia needed to wake up and get on top of this before a silly airport proposal took the focus of the *Dance* magazine story away from her dancing.

"Ladies." Sofia turned a performer's smile on the reporters, willing away her exhaustion with the steely determination that got her through seven-hour rehearsals. "I'm so sorry. I forgot I have a brief personal appointment. If you would be so kind as to give me a few moments?"

"Oh, but we've got such a good story going." The slim, delicately built reporter was surely a former dancer herself. She smiled with the same cobra-like grace of so many of Sofia's colleagues—a frightening show of sweetness that could precede a venomous strike. "Sofia, you never mentioned someone special in your life in our preliminary interview."

The camera turned toward the man who'd just proposed to her and the even more staggeringly handsome man beside him—another dark-haired, blue-eyed stranger, who wasn't as absurdly tall as her suitor. They had to be related. The second man's blue eyes were darker, frank and assessing. And he had a different kind of appeal from the well-muscled male dancers she worked with daily who honed their bodies for their art. Thicker in the shoulders and arms, he appeared strong enough to lift multiple ballerinas at once. With ease.

Tearing her eyes from him, she pushed aside the wayward thoughts. Then she promised the reporter the best incentive she could think of to obtain the respite she needed.

"If I can have a few moments to speak privately with my friend, you can film my audition for Idris Fortier." Sofia recalled the magazine had been angling for a connection to the famous choreographer. As much as she didn't want that moment on public record—especially if she failed to capture the lead role—she needed to get those cameras switched off now.

Her father wasn't going to run this show.

After a quick exchange of glances, the reporter with the camera lowered the lens and the pair retreated to a leather sofa in the almost empty waiting area. In the meantime, the rest of the troupe who had traveled with Sofia lingered.

"May we have a moment, ladies?" her father asked the bunch. And though some pouting followed, they went and joined the reporters, leaving Sofia and her father with the tall man, still holding a ring box, and his even more handsome relation.

Belatedly she realized she had mindlessly taken the orchids the stranger had offered her. She could only imagine how she looked in the pictures and video already captured by the magazine's photographer.

The same woman her publicist warned her moonlighted for the paparazzi. How fast would her story make the rounds?

"Sofia." The tall man leaned forward into her line of vision. "I'm Cameron McNeill. I hope our matchmaker let you know I'd be here to take you home?" Even now, he didn't lower his voice, but he had a puzzled expression.

She resisted the urge to glare at her father, afraid the reporter could use a long range-lens to film this conversation. Instead, Sofia gestured to some couches far removed from the others, but her suitor didn't budge as he studied her.

His companion, still watching her with those assessing blue eyes, said something quietly in the tall man's ear. A warning? A note of caution? He surreptitiously checked his phone.

"How do I know that name? McNeill?" Her father's chin jutted forward in challenge.

"Dad, please." After a life on stage studying the nuances of expressions to better emote in dance, Sofia knew how easily body language could tell a story. Especially to her fellow dancers. "May I?" Without waiting for an answer she turned back to Cameron. "Could we sit down for a moment?"

Her father snapped his fingers before anyone moved.

"McNeill Resorts?"

As soon as he uttered the words, the quiet man at Cameron's shoulder stepped forward with an air of command. He seemed a more approachable six foot two, something she could guess easily given the emphasis on paring the right dance partners in the ballet. Sofia's tired mind couldn't help a moment's romantic thought that this man would be a better fit for her. Purely from a dance perspective, of course.

He wore the overcoat and suit of a well-heeled Wall Street man, she thought. Yet there was a glint in his midnight-blue eyes, a fierceness she recognized as a subtler brand of passion.

Like hers.

"Vitaly Koslov?" Just by stepping forward into the small, awkward group, he somehow took charge. "I'm Quinn McNeill. We spoke briefly at the Met Gala two years ago."

A brother, she thought.

A very enticing brother. One who hadn't approached her with a marriage proposal in front of a journalist's camera. She approved of him more already, even as she wondered what these McNeill men were about.

She needed to think quickly and carefully.

"Sofia's got family in New York," Cameron informed Quinn, as if picking up a conversation they'd been in the middle of. "I knew she wasn't some kind of mail-order bride." He smiled down at Sofia with a grin too practiced for her taste. "The reporters must be doing some kind of story on you? I saw their media badges were from *Dance* magazine."

"Mail-order bride?" Her father's raised voice made even a few seen-it-all New Yorkers turn to stare, if only for a second. "I'll sue your family from here to Sunday, McNeill, if you're insinuating—"

"I knew she wasn't looking for a green card," Cameron argued, pulling out his phone while Sofia wished she could start this day all over again. "It was Quinn who thought that our meeting was a scam. But I got her picture from my matchmaker—"

"There's been a mix-up." Quinn stood between the two men, making her grateful she hadn't pulled the referee duty herself. "I told my brother as much before we realized who Sofia was."

Sofia couldn't decide if she was more incensed that she'd been mistaken for a bride for hire or that one of them wanted to marry her based on a photo. But frustration was building and the walls damn well had ears. She peered around nervously.

"Who is she?" Cameron asked Quinn, setting the conspicuous velvet box on a nearby table. Sofia felt all the eyes of her fellow dancers drawn to it like a magnet even from halfway across the waiting area.

"Sofia Koslov, principal dancer with the New York City Ballet." He passed Cameron his phone. He'd pulled up her photo and bio—she recognized it from the company web site. "Her father is the founder of Self-Sale, the online auction house, and one of the most powerful voices in Ukraine, where I'm trying to purchase that historic hotel."

The two brothers exchanged a meaningful look, clearly wary of her father's international influence.

While Cameron whistled softly and swiped a finger along the device's screen, Sofia's father looked ready to launch across the sofa and strangle him. Maybe her dad was regretting his choice of matchmaker already. Sofia certainly regretted his arrogant assumption that he could arrange her private life to suit him.

"You call that a *mix-up*?" Her father's accent thickened, a sure sign he was angry. "Why the hell would you think she needed a green card when she is an American citizen?" Her father articulated his words with an edge as he got in Quinn McNeill's face. "Do you have any idea how quickly I can bury your hotel purchase if I choose to, McNeill? If you think I'm going to let this kind of insult slide—"

"Of course not." Quinn didn't flinch. "We'll figure out something—"

Sofia missed the rest of the exchange as Cameron leaned closer to speak to her.

"You're really a ballerina?" He asked the question kindly enough, but there was a wariness in his eyes that Sofia had seen many times from people who equated "ballerina" with "prima donna." Or "diva."

"Yes." She lifted her chin, feeling defensive and wondering if Quinn could overhear them as he continued to speak in low tones with her father. The older brother drew her eye in a way men seldom did. And was it her tired imagination or did his gaze return to her often, as well? "I competed for years to move into a top position with one of the most rigorous and respected companies in the world."

Men never apologized for focusing on their careers. Why should she?

Cameron nodded but made no comment. She sensed him rethinking his marriage proposal in earnest. Not that it mattered—obviously a wedding wasn't happening. But how to dig herself out of this mess for the sake of the cameras and her peers? If she wasn't so drained from the long flight and the demanding practice schedule of this tour, maybe her brain would come up with a plausible, graceful way to extricate herself.

She noticed the members of her dance troupe moving steadily closer, no doubt trying to overhear what was going on in this strange powwow. Every last one of them had their phones in hand. She could almost imagine the tweets.

Will Sofia Koslov be too busy with her new fiancé to give her full attention to Fortier?

The dance world would go nuts. A flurry of speculation would ensue. Would Fortier decide he didn't want to work with a woman who didn't devote all of her free time to dance?

Her stomach cramped as she went cold inside. That would be so incredibly unfair. But it didn't take much to lose a lead role. It was all about what Fortier wanted.

"And you were not actively seeking a husband?" Cameron asked the question with a straight face.

Did he not realize she'd forgotten him completely? Her eyes ventured over to Quinn, hoping the man truly had an idea about how to fix this, the way he'd assured her father.

"No," she told him honestly. "I didn't even know my father had hired a matchmaker until shortly before we landed. He signed me up without permission."

"Then I apologize, Ms. Koslov, if I've caused you any embarrassment in my haste to find a bride." Cameron lifted her hand and put it to his lips, planting a kiss on the back of her knuckles. The gesture had the flair of a debonair flirt rather than any real sentiment. "My brother warned me not to rush into this. And, once again, it seems the ever-practical Quinn had a good point."

He straightened as if to leave, making her realize she would be on her own to explain this to the reporters. And the dance community. But she didn't blame Cameron. She blamed her father.

"You were really willing to marry someone without even talking to them?" She couldn't imagine what would drive him to propose to a stranger out of the blue.

"I was leaving it in the hands of professionals." He shrugged. "But next time, I will at least call the bride ahead of time. Good luck with your dancing, Sofia." He stuffed his hands into his coat pockets. "Quinn's flight doesn't take off for a few hours. If you need help with the reporters, my brother has a gift for keeping a cool head. He'll know what to do."

"You're…leaving?"

"I only came to the airport to see you. It's Quinn who has a flight out." He nodded toward his brother, who had captured the full attention of her father. "But he'll come up with a plan to help you with the reporters first. He's the expert at making the McNeills look good. I'm the brother who seems to stir up all the trouble."

It didn't occur to her to stop Cameron McNeill as he pivoted and stalked away from her, the necks of her traveling companions all craning to follow his progress through the airport terminal. She noticed other women doing the same thing.

But then, these McNeill men were uncommonly handsome.

The whole thing felt too surreal. And now the two reporters turned from the large windows on the other side of the terminal and headed her way again. The sick feeling returned in the pit of her stomach. She should have been using this time to come up with a plan. Maybe she could tell the reporters that the proposal had all been a joke?

Except she'd trip over any story she tried to concoct. Unlike her PR consultant, Sofia was not a master of putting the right spin on things. Besides, her colleagues' words about her not dating still circled around in her head.

About her lack of passion.

What would they say now that her suitor had ditched her publicly?

Her father and Quinn McNeill converged on her.

"You should listen, Sofia. McNeill has a fair plan." Vitaly nodded his satisfaction at whatever they'd decided.

Fear spiked in her chest as the reporters drew closer. These men didn't understand her world or the backlash this little drama would cause. How could she win the part in the Fortier ballet while her whole dance company gossiped gleefully about her five-minute marriage offer?

"No. I will handle this." She looked to Quinn McNeill. "I need to save face. To come up with something that doesn't make it look like I've been jilted—" Hell, she didn't know what she needed. She couldn't even explain herself to Quinn. How would she ever make sense in front of the reporters?

Quinn's blue eyes gave away exactly nothing. Whereas his younger brother was all charm and flirtation, this man's level stare was impossible to read. He seemed at ease, however. He leaned closer to her to speak softly while her father discreetly checked his watch, positioning himself between her and the oncoming dancers.

"Your father is livid at my brother's antics." Quinn's voice was like a warm stroke against her ear. It gave her a pleasant shiver in spite of her nervousness. "I'd like to appease him, but it's more important to me that you're not embarrassed by this. How can I help?"

She blurted the first thing that came to mind. "Ideally, I'd like a fiancé for the next three weeks until I have a ballet part on lockdown." As soon as the words tumbled out, of course, she realized that was impossible. Cameron McNeill was already gone.

But Quinn did not look deterred. He nodded.

"Whatever I say, please know that it's just for show." His hand landed on her spine, a heated touch that seeped right through her mohair cape. "We'll give a decoy statement to the media and then you and I can iron out some kind of formal press release afterward. But I can have you happily engaged and out of here in less than five minutes. Just follow my lead."

She didn't even have time to meet his eyes and see for herself his level of sincerity, because the cameras were rolling again, the bright light in her eyes. Excited whispering from the other dancers provided an uncomfortable background music for whatever performance Quinn McNeill was about to give.

Strange that, when her reputation hung in the balance, the main thing she noticed was how his hand palmed the small of her back with a surety and command even a dancing master would appreciate.

Her father hung back as the flashing red light on the Nikon handheld swung her way. Blinking while her eyes adjusted, she thought she saw her father reclaim the velvet ring box Cameron had left behind and hand it to Quinn. Which made sense, she supposed. The brother of empty gestures left a diamond behind while the practical brother reclaimed it. Hadn't

Cameron assured her Quinn would take care of everything?

"Ladies." Quinn's voice took on a very different quality as he turned to the camera and the small audience of her colleagues who clutched their cell phones, surely eager to send out updates on this little drama. "Forgive me for spiriting away Sofia earlier. In my eagerness to see her again, I failed to remember her interview with the magazine. I didn't mean for a private moment to be caught on film."

Sofia could almost hear the collective intake of breath. Or was that her own? Her stomach twisted, fearing what he might say next while at the same time she couldn't make herself interrupt. Like any strong partner, he led with authority.

Besides, he said it was only for show.

"Where is your brother?" one of the reporters asked. "He said he couldn't wait to meet his bride."

No doubt they'd all been surfing the internet to figure out who Cameron and Quinn were.

"My brother was teasing. Cameron hadn't met Sofia yet and, in the way brothers sometimes do..." He deployed a charming grin of his own, one even more disarming than his brother's had been, only now she realized how practiced the gesture could be. "Cam only said that to rattle me on the day he knew I was going to ask her something very important myself."

Quinn turned to her now, his blue eyes locking on her with an intensity that speared right down to her belly to stir an unexpected heat. Even when she knew with one hundred percent certainty it was all an act.

"He just so happened to have a ring in his pocket?" the reporter asked, gaze narrowed to search out the truth.

"I had no idea he brought an old ring of our mother's from home," Quinn continued easily. "Then he grabbed some flowers from the customer service desk." He pointed out a half-empty vase nearby. "Trust me when I tell you, my brother doesn't lack for a sense of humor—a somewhat twisted one."

Even Sofia found herself wondering about his story. Quinn looked convincing enough, especially when he gazed down at her as if she was the only woman in the world.

She licked her lips, her mouth gone suddenly dry. She should say something. Prevent this farce that no one would ever believe. But then again…hadn't she promised herself she would make this a performance worth watching?

A show of passion?

"Now—" his gaze never left hers even as he continued to address the media "—I am going to ask you to check Ms. Koslov's schedule for a new interview time tomorrow. Because tonight, we have something private and wonderful to celebrate."

Somewhere behind that bright light the camerawoman gave a quiet squeal of excitement while someone else—a colleague from the ballet company, no doubt—made a huff of disappointment. That the story hadn't panned out how she'd wanted? Or that she'd have to wait until tomorrow for answers? A few people clapped halfheartedly. The dancers who had hoped for a scandal were clearly disappointed while Sofia wondered how she'd ever dared to ask Quinn McNeill for a temporary fiancé. She couldn't believe he'd granted her wish.

And not with his brother but with Quinn himself as her fake groom.

The cameras captured every moment of this absurd dance as she clutched the bouquet in one hand while Quinn tucked the mysterious black-velvet box into the other. Then, leaving no doubt as to his meaning, he slanted his lips overs hers and kissed her.

Three

Normally, Quinn McNeill knew how to stick to the talking points. He'd delivered enough unwelcome news to investors during his father's failed tenure as the McNeill Resorts' CEO that Quinn had a knack for staying on script.

But all bets were off, it seemed, when an exotic beauty fit into his arms as if she'd been made for him. One moment he'd been delivering the cover story to explain Cam's behavior and still give Sofia Koslov a fiancé. The next, he was drowning in her wide gray eyes, her full lips luring him into a minty-flavored kiss that made the mayhem of the airport fade away.

This was so not the plan he'd come up with to smooth over business relations with Sofia's ticked-off and powerful Ukrainian father. He'd told Vitaly

Koslov he would publicly apologize and explain away the proposal as a joke between friends. But when Quinn had seen the panic on Sofia's face, he'd known his only option was to help her in whatever way she needed.

Although, it occurred to him as he kissed her...

What if she'd meant she wanted that fake engagement with his brother?

Forcing himself to edge back slowly, Quinn peered down at her kissed-plump lips and flushed cheeks. She couldn't have possibly meant she wanted anything to do with Cameron. Not after that kiss.

Still, he'd just complicated things a whole lot by claiming her as his own.

"So you're engaged to Ms. Koslov?" one of the reporters asked him while the other one flipped off the power button on her camera.

"A full statement will be issued tomorrow morning," Vitaly Koslov snapped before Quinn could respond, the older man's patience clearly worn thin as he shot a dark glare at Quinn.

The hotel deals he was working on in Kiev and Prague were now seriously compromised. The man had threatened to block the sales by any means necessary if Quinn didn't smooth things over with the media, and Quinn was guessing that taking Cameron's place as Sofia's suitor wasn't what Vitaly Koslov had in mind.

Right now, however, Quinn had promised the man to get his daughter out of the terminal and home as quickly and privately as possible.

"Come with me," Quinn whispered in Sofia's ear, a few strands of silky hair brushing his cheek as he bent to shoulder her bag for her. "Your father will divert them. We are too happy and in love to pay attention to anyone else."

He started walking toward the exit, hoping she would continue to play her part in this charade. She did just that, moving with quick, efficient steps and glancing up at him in a way that was more than just affectionate.

Hell. Those gazes sizzled.

"How fortunate we are," she muttered dryly. Her tone was at odds with the way she was looking at him, making him realize what a skilled actress she was.

Had the kiss been for show, too? He liked to think he could tell the difference.

"I regret that we have to do this. I hope my brother at least had the decency to apologize before he made his escape." Quinn had already texted his pilot to reschedule his own flight, a delay that would add to the considerable expense of closing this deal that might never happen anyhow.

He held the door for Sofia and flagged the first limo he spotted, handing off her luggage to the driver to stow. The wind plastered her cape to Quinn's legs, bringing with it the faint scent of a subtle perfume.

"He did apologize." She tucked the mohair wrap tighter around herself, waiting on the curb while the driver opened the door and she relayed the address of her apartment. "He told me he was sorry right before he assured me you'd take care of everything." She slid to the far side of the vehicle, distancing herself from him. "Tell me, Quinn, how often do you step in to claim his discarded fiancées?"

He understood that she was frustrated, so he told himself not to be defensive.

"This would be a first," he replied lightly, taking the seat on the opposite side of the limo. "I tried to talk him out of hunting for a wife in this drastic manner, but he was determined."

The driver was already behind the wheel and steering the vehicle toward the exit. Darkness had fallen while they were inside the terminal.

"It would not have been so awkward if there hadn't been any media present." She seemed to relax a bit as she leaned deeper into the leather seat, pulling the pink scarf off her neck to wrap it around one hand. "Then again, maybe it would have been since I had the rest of the dance ensemble with me and there are those who would love nothing more than a chance to undermine my position in the company."

"Your father told me that you were recently promoted to principal." He only had a vague knowledge of the ballet, having attended a handful of events for social purposes. "Does that always put a target on a dancer's back?"

"Only if your name is mentioned for a highly sought-after part in a new ballet to premiere next year. Or if you rise through the ranks too quickly. Or if your father sponsors a gala fund-raiser and angles for you to be featured prominently in the program." She wound the scarf around her other hand, weaving it through her fingers. "Then, no matter how talented you are, the rumor persists that you only achieved your position because of money."

In the glow from the streetlights, he watched her delicate wrists as she anxiously fumbled with the scarf. She hadn't been this skittish back in the airport. Did he make her nervous? Or was she only allowing herself the show of nerves now that she was out of the spotlight?

He found himself curious about her even though he should be focusing on the details of their brief, pretend engagement and not ruminating on her life. Her kiss.

"You move in a competitive world." It was something he understood from the business he managed outside of McNeill Resorts since his bigger income stream came from his work as a hedge fund manager. His every financial move was watched and dissected by his rivals and second-guessed by nervous investors.

"The competition led me to hire a PR firm at my own expense, which is costly, considering a dancer's salary. But they secured the feature for me in *Dance* magazine."

He had no idea what a professional ballerina earned, but the idea that she'd hired a publicity firm suggested a strong investment in her career. Quinn found it intriguing that she would pay for that herself considering her father's wealth.

That wasn't all he found intriguing. The spike of attraction he felt for her—a heat that had intensified with that kiss—surprised him. He'd been adamantly opposed to his grandfather's marriage ultimatum and yet he'd found himself jumping into the fray today to claim Sofia for his own.

Not just for McNeill Resorts. Also so Cameron couldn't have her.

As soon as he'd seen her today, he'd felt an undeniable sexual interest. No, hunger.

"I realize that my brother created an awkward situation and you have every right to be frustrated."

"And yet you helped me out of a tricky situation when I was tongue-tied and nervous, so thank you for that." She settled her hands in her lap and stared out the window at the businesses lining either side of Interstate 17 heading south toward Manhattan. "I have a difficult audition ahead of me and I know I wouldn't have been able to focus on it if the debacle in the airport was the topic on everyone's lips." She gave him a half smile. "If I didn't have a fiancé, everyone would badger me about what happened. But since I actually *do*? I don't think anyone will quiz me about it. Sadly, my competitors are more interested in my failures than my successes."

He understood. He just hoped her father would support her wishes regarding their charade.

"Yet tonight's events leave you a loophole, Sofia, if you want to give a statement that you refused me." He hadn't thought about it until now, but just because he'd implied he was asking for her hand didn't mean she would necessarily accept. "If you change your mind about this, I can have someone work on a statement for the press that expresses my admiration for you, my disappointment in your refusal—"

"Expedient for you, but not for me." She tipped her head to the window, her expression weary. He noticed the pale purple shadows beneath her eyes. "Just because I issue a statement that says it's over doesn't mean there won't be questions about my love life given the backstabbing in my company this season. An abrupt breakup when everyone wants a story could make the press start digging into how we met. And until I know the truth about where Cameron got my contact information, I'm not comfortable letting the media look too closely at how we connected. I never wanted anything to do with a matchmaker, and I'm concerned that whoever my father hired posted my information in a misleading way. I don't understand why your brother thought I was Ukrainian. Or why he didn't know I was a dancer."

"We could work on a cover story—"

"I am exhausted and my body thinks it's midnight after the time I spent in Kiev. I have rehearsal tomorrow at ten and what I need is sleep, not a late-night study session to keep a cover story straight." She folded her arms and squared her shoulders, as if readying herself for an argument.

Did she realize how many complications would arise if they continued this fictional engagement? He'd really thought she would jump at the chance to say she'd turned down his proposal. But then again, he couldn't deny a surge of desire at the prospect of seeing her again.

"I'm willing to continue with the appearance of an engagement if that's simpler for you." He wanted to right the mess Cameron had made. And this time, it wasn't for Cameron's sake.

It was for Sofia's.

"It would be easier for me." She twisted some of her windblown blond hair behind her ear and he noticed a string of five tiny pearls outlining the curve. "Just for three more weeks. A month, at most, until the rumor mill in my company settles down. I need to get through that important audition."

She glanced his way for the first time in miles and caught him staring.

"Of course," he agreed, mentally recalibrating his schedule to accommodate a woman in his life. He would damn well hand off the trip to Kiev to Cameron or Ian since Quinn would need to remain in New York. "In that case, maybe we should draw up a contract outlining the terms of the arrangement."

With Vitaly Koslov threatening to block his business in Eastern Europe, Quinn needed to handle this as carefully as he would any complicated foreign acquisition.

"Is that wise?" Frowning, she withdrew a tin of mints from her leather satchel and fished a couple out, offering him one. "A paper trail makes it easier for someone to discover our secret."

He took a mint, his eye drawn to her mouth as her lips parted. He found himself thinking about that kiss again. The way she'd tasted like mint then, too. And how an engagement would lead to more opportunities to touch her. The idea of a fake fiancée didn't feel like an imposition when he looked at it that way. Far from it.

"Quinn?" Her head tipped sideways as she studied him, making him realize he'd never responded. "If you really think we need the protection of a legally binding contract—"

"Not necessarily." He should keep this light. Friendly. Functional. "But we'll want to be sure both of our interests are protected and that we know what we're getting into."

"A prenup for a false engagement." She shook her head. "Only in New York."

"Your father will want to ensure your reputation emerges unscathed," he reminded her.

The limo driver hit the brakes suddenly, making them both lurch forward. On instinct, Quinn's arm went out, restraining her. It was purely protective, until that moment when he became aware of his forearm pinned against her breasts, his hand anchored to her shoulder under the fall of silky hair.

A soft flush stole over her cheeks as he released her and they each settled back against their respective seat cushions. The awkward moment and the unwelcome heat seemed to mock his need to put the terms of this relationship in writing.

"That's fine," she agreed quickly, as if she couldn't end the conversation fast enough. "If you want to draw up something, I will sign it and you can be sure I will not cause a fuss when we end the engagement."

She wrapped her mohair cape more tightly around

her slight figure, the action only reminding him of her graceful curves and the way she'd felt against him.

Damn. His body acted as though it'd been months since he'd been with a woman when...

Now that he thought about it, maybe it had been that long since he'd ended a relationship with Portia, the real-estate developer who'd tried to sell him a Park Avenue penthouse. In the end, Quinn hadn't been ready to leave the comfort of the Pierre, a hotel he'd called home for almost a decade. He hadn't been ready for Portia, either, who'd been more interested in being a New York power couple than she had been in him.

Somehow he'd avoided dating since then and that had been...last year. Hell. No wonder the slightest brush of bodies was making him twitchy. Gritting his teeth against the surge of hunger, he told himself to stay on track. Focused. To clean up his brother's mess and move on.

The sooner they got through the next month, the better.

Sofia breathed through the attraction the same way she'd exhale after a difficult turn. She ignored the swirl of distracting sensations, calling on a lifetime's worth of discipline.

She controlled her body, not the other way around. And she most definitely would not allow handsome Quinn McNeill to rattle her with his touch. Or with his well-timed kisses that were just for show, even if the one she'd experienced had felt real enough.

With an effort, she steered him back toward their conversation, needing his captivating eyes to be on something besides her.

"I'm curious about the plan you developed with my father. I'm certain it didn't involve us being engaged." She would rather know before her father contacted her. Her powerful parent would never stop interfering with her life, insisting he knew best on everything from which public relations firm should promote her career to hiring a matchmaker she didn't want.

They'd butted heads on everything since her mother had died of breast cancer during Sofia's teens, ending her independence and putting her under the roof of a cold, controlling man. Until then, she and her mother had lived a bohemian lifestyle all over the US and Europe, her mom painting while she danced. When her mother died, she'd been too young to strike out alone and her father had been determined to win her over with his wealth and the opportunities it could afford.

She'd wanted no part of it. Until he'd found that magic carrot—ballet school in St. Petersburg, Russia, an opportunity she truly couldn't ignore. But she'd been paying for the privilege in so many ways since then, her debt never truly repaid.

"He wanted me to write off Cam's behavior as a private joke between old friends." Quinn shifted conversational gears easily. "But I'm sure he'll be glad that your preferences were considered."

"Vitaly has never concerned himself with my preferences." She already dreaded the phone call from

him she knew was coming. He would be angry with
her, for certain. But she needed to remind him that
he wasn't the injured party here. "But he is not the
only one affected by his decision to hire a matchmaker without my permission. I need to call him and
demand he have that contract terminated immediately. I don't want my photo and profile posted anywhere else."

"Would you like me to tell him?" Quinn asked.
She must have appeared surprised because he quickly
added, "I don't mean to overstep. But he and I have
unfinished business and I plan to find out exactly
where Cameron found your profile. I'm not sure who
is at fault for the miscommunication between your
matchmaker and his, but I plan to look into it as a
matter of legal protection for McNeill Resorts since
your father threatened to sue at one point."

Sofia sighed. "I'm ninety percent sure that was
just blustering, but I honestly don't blame you. And
since I'd rather not speak to my father when I'm so
upset with him, I'd actually be grateful if you would
handle it."

It was a sad commentary on her relationship with
her father that, while she hardly knew Quinn, she
was already certain he would deal with her dad more
effectively.

"Consider it done. And for what it's worth, he
seemed to care a great deal about you when I spoke
with him." Quinn said the words carefully. Diplomati-
cally. No wonder Cameron relied on him to take care
of sticky situations. "But I'm most concerned about

your expectations going forward." He narrowed his gaze as he turned back toward her. "For instance, how often we need to be seen together in public. If we're going to do this, we'll need to coordinate dates and times."

"Really?" She was too tired and overwhelmed by the events of the evening to maintain the pragmatic approach now that it was just the two of them. "Although it's been a while since I dated, I'm sure that we managed to schedule outings without a lot of pre-planning. Why don't I just text you tomorrow?"

His short bark of laughter surprised her as the limo descended into the Lincoln Tunnel toward Manhattan. Shadows crossed his face in quick succession in spite of the tinted windows.

"Fair enough. But maybe we could find a time to speak tomorrow. I'd like to be sure we agree on a story about how we met since you'll be talking to the media."

A stress headache threatened just from thinking about how carefully she would have to walk through that minefield, but damn it, she'd worked too hard to land that feature in *Dance* magazine to allow her pretend love life to steal all the spotlight.

"I have a rehearsal tomorrow at ten and I'll be jet-lagged and foggy-headed before that." She could barely think straight now to hammer out the details. "What if I just avoid reporters until we speak later in the day?"

Tomorrow's challenges would be difficult enough. She couldn't believe she'd also offered for *Dance* magazine to film her private audition with Idris Fortier the following week. She would be stressed enough that day without having her mistakes captured on video.

"This news might travel fast." He frowned, clearly disliking the idea of waiting. "But I understand about jet lag making conversation counterproductive in the morning. Can I pick you up after rehearsal then?"

His voice slid past her defenses for a moment; the question was the kind of thing a lover might ask her. Was it certifiable to spend so much time with him this month? He was the antithesis of the kind of men she normally dated—artists and bohemians who moved in vastly different worlds from the Koslov family dynasty. Quinn, on the other hand, was the kind of polished, powerful captain of industry who liked to rule the world according to his whim. The tendency was apparent from the moment he'd strode into her personal drama today and quietly taken over.

His assistance had been valuable, without question. But would she regret letting herself get close to a man like that? Especially one with such unexpected appeal?

"After rehearsal will work." She steadied herself as the limo driver jammed on the gas, trying to make some headway down Fifth Avenue despite the rush-hour traffic. "I'll be done by four. Do you know where the theater is?"

"Of course." He shifted his long legs in front of him, his open overcoat brushing her thigh when he moved. "Is there a side door? Somewhere to make a more discreet exit?"

She crossed her legs, shifting away from him.

"Good idea. There's a coffee shop on Columbus Avenue." She checked the address on her phone and shared it with him as the car finally turned down Ninth Street in the East Village where she lived. Her phone continued to vibrate every few minutes, reminding her that the whole world would have questions for her in the morning.

"Do you live alone?" he asked as the car rolled to a stop outside her building.

The question shouldn't surprise her since the neighborhood wasn't the kind of place where hedge fund managers made their home. Her father hated this place, routinely trying to entice her into rooms at the Plaza or a swank Park Avenue place.

"Yes." Her spine straightened as if she was standing in front of the ballet barre. "I love it here."

He got out of the car to walk her to the door while the driver retrieved her bag. In the time it took her to find her keys in her purse, two older men stumbled out of a local bar, boisterous and loud. She noticed that Quinn kept an eye on them until they passed the entrance to her building.

"Thanks for the ride." She opened the front door and stood in the entryway, very ready to dive into bed.

Alone, obviously. Although the thought of diving into bed with Quinn sent a warm wave of sexual interest through her.

"I'm walking you to your apartment door," he insisted, eyes still scanning the street out front that was filled with more bars than residences.

Too weary to argue, she gave a clipped nod and led the way through the darkened corridor toward the elevator. She was vaguely aware that he had taken her bags from the limo driver and was carrying them for her. A few moments later, arriving at apartment 5C, Quinn stepped inside long enough to settle her luggage in the narrow foyer. Strange how much smaller her apartment seemed with him in it. She watched as his blue gaze ran over the row of pendant lamps illuminating the dark hardwood floor and white grasscloth walls covered with dozens of snapshots of ballet performances and backstage photos.

Maybe it was a sudden moment of self-consciousness that made her grab her cell phone when it vibrated again for what seemed like the tenth time in as many minutes. Checking the screen, she realized the incoming texts weren't from curious colleagues or her father.

Half were from the publicity firm she'd hired. The other half were from the ballet mistress. A quick scan of the content told her they were all concerned about the same thing—social media speculation had suggested she wasn't serious about the Fortier ballet and was focusing on her personal life. She felt her muscles tighten and tense as if she were reading a review of a subpar performance, the stress twisting along her shoulders and squeezing her temples.

"Is everything all right?" Quinn's voice seemed

distant compared to the imagined shout of the all-caps text messages.

"You were right. News of our engagement traveled quickly." Swallowing hard, she set the phone on an antique cabinet near the door. "My publicist urged me to wear an engagement band tomorrow to forestall questions until she writes the press release." Anger blazed through her in a fresh wave, shaking her out of her exhaustion. "It is a sad statement on my achievements that a lifetime of hard work is overshadowed by a rich man's proposal."

She wrenched off her scarf and fumbled with the buttons on her cape, anger making her movements stiff.

"It's because of your achievements that anyone is interested in your private life," Quinn reminded her quietly, reaching for the oversize buttons and freeing them.

She might have protested his sudden nearness, but in an instant he was already behind her, lifting the mohair garment from her shoulders to hang it on the wrought-iron coatrack.

"It still isn't fair," she fumed, although she could feel some of her anger leaking away as Quinn's words sank into her agitated mind. He had a point. A surprisingly thoughtful one. "No man would ever be badgered to wear a wedding ring to quiet his colleagues about his romantic status."

"No." He dug into his coat pocket and took out the small, dark box that had caused such havoc at Teterboro. "But since you've been put in a tremendously awkward position, maybe we should see what Cameron had in mind for his proposal."

He held out the box. The absurdity of the night struck her again as she stared at it. Who would have suspected when she boarded her plane in Kiev so many hours ago that she would be negotiating terms of an engagement with a total stranger in her apartment before bedtime?

"Why not? It's not like I'm going to be able to sleep now with all this to worry me." Shrugging, she backed deeper into her apartment, flipping on a metal floor lamp arching over the black leather sofa. "Come in, if you like. I haven't been home in three weeks so it feels nice to see my own things. I'm glad to be home even if it has been a crazy day."

She gestured toward the couch, taking a seat on the vintage steamer trunk that served as a coffee table.

"Only for a minute." He didn't remove his coat, but he did drop down onto the black leather seat. "I know you must be ready for bed." Their eyes connected for the briefest of moments before he glanced back at the ring box. "But let's take a look."

He levered open the black-velvet top to reveal a ring that took her breath away.

Quinn whistled softly. "You're sure you never met my brother before today?"

"Positive." Her hand reached for the ring without her permission, the emerald-cut diamond glowing like a crystal ball lit from within. A halo of small diamonds surrounded the central one, and the double band glittered with still more of them. "It can't possibly be real with so many diamonds. Although it looks like platinum."

"It is platinum." He sounded certain. "My brother goes all-in when he makes a statement." Gently he pried the ring from the box. "And given how much trouble his statement caused you today, I think it's only fair you wear it tomorrow."

Dropping the box onto the couch cushion, he held the ring in one hand and took her palm in the other. The shock of his warm fingers on her skin caught her off guard.

"I can't wear that." She sat across from him, their knees bumping while his thumb rested in the center of her palm.

Awareness sparked deep inside her, a light, leaping feeling like a perfectly executed cabriolé jump. Her heart beat faster.

A slow smile stretched across Quinn's face, transforming his features from ruggedly handsome to swoon-worthy.

"We agreed on an engagement. Don't you think it makes more sense to use the ring we have than to go shopping for a new one?"

The insinuation that she was being impractical helped her to see past that dazzling smile.

"I never would have guessed your brother would spend a small fortune on a ring for a woman he never met." She edged out of his grip. "I thought he was a romantic, not completely certifiable."

Quinn's smile faded. "I assure you, Cameron is neither." He set the ring on the steamer trunk beside her. "I'll let you decide whether or not to wear it in the morning. And in the meantime, I'd better let you get some rest."

He rose to his feet, leaving a priceless piece of jewelry balanced on last month's *Vogue*.

"Quinn." She stood to follow him to the door then reached back to grab the ring so she could return it. "Please. I don't feel right keeping this here."

He turned to face her as he reached the door, but made no move to take the glittering ring.

"If you were my bride-to-be, I would spare no expense to show the world you were mine." His blue eyes glowed with a warmth that had her remembering his kiss. Her breath caught in her chest and she wondered what it might be like for him to call her that for real.

Mine.

"I'm—" *At a total loss for words.* "That is—" She folded the diamond into her hand, squeezing it tightly so the stones pressed into her soft skin, distracting her from her hypnotic awareness of this man. "If you insist."

"It's a matter of believability, Sofia."

"It's only for one month." She wasn't sure if she said it to remind him or herself.

"We'll work out the details tomorrow." He reached to smooth a strand of hair from her forehead, barely touching her and still sending shimmers of pleasure along her temple and all the way down the back of her neck. "Sleep well."

She didn't even manage to get her voice working

before he was out the door again, leaving her alone in a suddenly too empty apartment.

Squeezing the ring tighter in her fist, she waited for the pinch of pain from the sharp edges of the stones. She needed to remember that this wasn't real. Quinn McNeill had only agreed to this mad scheme to clean up his brother's mess. Any hint of attraction she felt needed to be squashed immediately, especially since Quinn was cut from the same mold as her father—focused on business and the accumulation of wealth. Her world was about art, emotions and human connections.

Her mother had taught her that people did not fall into both camps. In Sofia's experience it was true. And since she wanted her own relationships to be meaningful bonds rooted in shared creativity and ideals, she was willing to wait until she had more time in her life to find the right partner. Romance could not be rushed.

"It's only for a month," she said aloud again, forcing herself to set the engagement ring on the hallway table.

Surely she could keep up her end of a fake engagement for the sake of appearances? She'd made countless sacrifices for her career, from dancing on broken toes to living away from her family on the other side of the globe to train with Russian ballet masters.

Ignoring the sensual draw of Quinn McNeill couldn't possibly be more difficult than those challenges.

Yet, even as she marched herself off to bed, she

feared she was lying to herself that she could keep her hands off the man anywhere near as easily as she'd set down the ring.

Four

Quinn pulled an all-nighter, working straight through until noon the next day. He rearranged his schedule to accommodate more time in the city over the upcoming month. He'd avoided the office and shut off his phone for all but critical notifications, not ready to address the questions about his relationship with Sofia until they'd worked out a game plan.

Sofia.

Shoving away from the overly bright screen on his laptop, Quinn leaned back into the deep leather cushioning of his office chair. His grandfather's old chair, even after decades of use, seemed to retain class and grace, a steady touchstone in a career that constantly demanded invention and innovation to stay competitive. Eyes wandering to the corner of his walnut desk, he absently skimmed over the open newspaper. Even with news apps on his phone, Quinn still read the paper every morning, feeling a sense of connection to the ink and paper. And he couldn't ignore what was printed in today's society section—a photograph of the lithe ballerina.

She hadn't been far from his thoughts all morning and now was no different as he shut down his computer and headed out of the office building to his chauffeur-driven Escalade. And damn if Sofia didn't continue to dance through his mind as he rode toward the site of McNeill Resorts' latest renovation project in Brooklyn. Quinn powered down his laptop and stored it in the compartment beside the oversize captain's chair. He tried to prep himself for the inevitable confrontation with Cameron, who was slated to be on site in their grandfather's absence.

Even though his brother had walked away from his would-be ballerina bride yesterday, Quinn guessed that Cameron would still have something to say about the turn of events after he'd left. And though Quinn hoped he'd quelled some of Sofia's father's anger, he knew the engagement would make waves with his brother. If anything, Quinn hoped that this would make Cameron come to his senses about tying the knot with a woman he'd never met.

Running his hand through thick hair, Quinn let out a low sigh. He needed Cameron to be rational today.

He pressed the switch for the intercom as the Escalade rolled to a stop.

"I shouldn't be long, Jeff," Quinn told his driver

before he stepped out of the vehicle in front of the converted bank on Montague Street in Brooklyn Heights. Coffee in hand, he headed onto the site, his well-worn leather shoes crunching against the gravel and construction dust.

Glancing at the scaffolding on the building, he nodded at the progress as the smell of fresh-cut wood and the sounds of hammering filled the air.

"Morning, Giacomo." Quinn nodded to the site foreman before picking up a hard hat to enter the building.

Giacomo—a sought-after project manager who specialized in historic conversions—gave a silent wave, his ear pressed to his cell phone while he juggled a coffee and a tablet full of project notes. The guy pointed to the roof of the building, answering Quinn's unasked question about his brother's whereabouts. Out of respect, the only time the McNeills showed up at each other's job sites was to talk family business.

Or, in this case, family brides.

Mood darkening as he anticipated an argument, Quinn climbed the temporary stairs installed during the renovation stage to connect the floors that had been stripped down to the studs. A swirl of cement dust kicked up from some kind of demo work on the second floor, and he quickened his steps. He passed some workers perched on scaffolding outside the fourth floor, debating the merits of salvaging some of the crumbling granite façade. Quinn had practically grown up on job sites like this, frequently travelling around the country with his grandfather to learn the business.

At least, that had been the family's party line. The larger reason was that, during the six months of the year his father had custody of his sons, Liam McNeill was usually too busy thrill-seeking around the globe to bother with parental duties.

Cliff-jumping in Santorini, Greece, or white-water rafting down a perilous South Korean river always seemed like more fun to Quinn's father than child-rearing. So Malcolm McNeill had stepped in more times than not, teaching his grandsons about property development and the resort industry from the ground up.

Reaching the rooftop, Quinn spied his brother looking out at the skyline from the structure's best feature—a sunny oasis on the roof that would one day be a space for outdoor dining, drinks and special events. Even at noon the view was breathtaking. But at dusk, when the sun slipped behind the Manhattan skyline, there was no finer perspective on the city than right here.

Cameron sat in a beat-up plastic patio chair that looked like a Dumpster salvage, the legs speckled with various-colored paints. He had dragged the seat close to the edge of the roof, his laptop balanced on his knees and his hard hat sitting on a section of exposed trusses at his feet. His dark jeans sported sawdust, his leg bouncing to some unheard rhythm.

Quinn must have made a noise or cast a shadow because Cameron looked toward him.

"I'm not sure I want to see you right now." Cameron didn't smile, his attention returning to his computer screen. "The headlines I've seen so far don't exactly fill me with confidence about what went on last night after I left."

"The key point there being—you left." Quinn had never connected as well with Cam as he did with Ian, and that made it tougher to see Cameron's side now when his younger brother seemed so clearly in the wrong.

"So you felt compelled to stick around and play white knight?" Cameron flipped the screen of his laptop to face Quinn, showing a headline that read Two McNeill Magnates Propose to Former Sugarplum Fairy.

The accompanying photo showed Sofia pirouetting across a stage in a tutu. Damn. So he hadn't really imagined how hot she was. The levelheaded, practical side of Quinn reeled at the absurd headline and the media circus that would continue to send in the clowns until the official "engagement" story aired.

But his rational side didn't seem to be in full control. Sofia's petite body, her lean and limber pose, made him recall their kiss and the heat of that impromptu moment.

Cameron set his jaw, daggers dancing from his eyes. Accusatory and angry, sure. It was all Quinn needed to be drawn back to the problem at hand.

Quinn crossed his arms, undaunted. Cam had to realize what was at stake.

"You piss off her father, one of the wealthiest men

in the world, who also happens to have enough Eastern European connections to run our deal for the new resorts into the ground, and call it none of my business?" Quinn shook his head and dragged a crate over to where Cameron was sitting. He planted a foot on it.

Cameron's mouth thinned, his voice a near growl. "You crossed a line into my personal affairs and you know it. You don't just propose to your brother's girl five minutes after they're through." Cameron tipped back in the plastic chair like it was a rocker. It teetered on two legs.

The move put Quinn's teeth on edge but not nearly as much as his words. Cam would think no more of walking across exposed truss beams at two stories than he would at twelve.

"Sofia was never yours," Quinn reminded him, more irritated than he ought to be at the idea, as a protective fire suddenly blazed in the pit of his chest. "And you lost any chance you had of salvaging something with her when you walked out of the airport yesterday."

For once, however, Quinn couldn't be disappointed with in Cam's impulsive ways. The thought of her sharing that kiss with anyone but Quinn was intolerable.

"Think what you want of my motives, but I saw how you were looking at her." Cameron drummed his fingers along the back of the laptop case.

That stopped him. He couldn't deny that he'd felt something as soon as he'd seen her in person.

Cam shook his head. "And I still wouldn't have

walked out, except I saw her looking at you that same exact way. It's one thing for me to turn my back on a bar fight or a heated investors meeting, but, contrary to popular belief, I wouldn't leave the woman to fend off nosy journalists if I hadn't seen the looks darting back and forth between you two."

"In that case…thank you." Stunned by a depth of insight he'd never given his brother credit for, Quinn wasn't sure how to handle the new information. Had Sofia been as drawn to him as he was to her? "After speaking to her father, I'm beginning to think her privacy was compromised by the matchmaker he hired. Bad enough Vitaly Koslov contracted the consultant without her knowledge. But I don't think he would have ever sanctioned his daughter's photo and contact information on the kind of pick-a-bride profile site you described to me."

"I thought the same thing after I left the airport yesterday." Cameron turned his laptop screen so Quinn could see the web banner for a Manhattan matchmaker, Mallory West. "I called my own matchmaker and she reminded me that I knowingly chose a match off a third-party web site Mallory West's clients can access, so I was informed ahead of time that Ms. West didn't know those women personally. She simply facilitated the meet. She gave me a full refund and assured me she would speak to the person who vetted the women on the web site I viewed."

Quinn sank down onto the crate and looked out across the bay on the sprawl of Lower Manhattan anchored by the Freedom Tower. Now that he'd seen firsthand how much havoc Cameron's bride hunt had caused for Sofia, he was thoroughly invested in the whole debacle.

"How can a matchmaker match people she doesn't actually know?" That sounded unethical. "I didn't think that's how they worked."

Cameron nodded as he signed into a private web page.

"They don't. But I was in a hurry and didn't want to jump through a lot of hoops since I wasn't really looking for true love everlasting." Cameron shrugged. "And Mallory's right—she was just a facilitator. I was paying special attention to the women listed on that third-party web site."

"Defeating the whole purpose of a matchmaker." Quinn ground his teeth together. "You might as well have gone shopping for a bride online. Why the hell would you pay the rates for a private matchmaker only to meet a woman whose name you pulled out of a damn hat?"

Cam seemed to take the question seriously. "I wanted to speed up the process and I hoped that the matchmaker's résumé lent credibility to the women I met."

Quinn wished he'd paid better attention when Cameron had first told him about his visit to the matchmaker's office, but at the time, he'd been focused on talking Cam out of jumping into a marriage.

"So she's taking no responsibility and she gave you your money back, which makes me wonder if she's worried about that web site, too. Can you still access that page?"

"No. Now that I've given up my membership with Mallory West, I can't, but Ms. West said Sofia's profile is no longer included on the page."

"And once you told her you were interested in meeting Sofia, she texted you the flight details?"

"Correct." Cameron closed the laptop.

"I'll pass that information along to Sofia's father. I'm hoping to defuse some of his anger. After all, he was the one who released her photo in the first place. It's not your fault he hired an incompetent matchmaker." Quinn raised his voice as a jackhammer went to work somewhere in the building. The roof vibrated with the noise.

"I find it ironic that I ran out to marry a woman because of Gramps' will, and Sofia was my match based on her father's equally manipulative tactics to see her wed." Cameron picked up his hard hat and juggled it from one hand to another, his eyes never leaving some distant point to the northwest.

"Right. But I don't understand why Vitaly was surprised to see you in the airport if he shared the flight information with Sofia's matchmaker, who shared it with yours." Quinn's teeth rattled as the vibrations under his feet picked up strength. "I don't think his surprise was an act. Which means something doesn't add up."

He'd already hired a guy in his company's IT department to research any information about Sofia Koslov that had been posted online in the last month.

Even if the third-party web site had deleted her profile, this guy could usually find reliable traces. For Quinn, it would help to show Vitaly where Cameron had found Sofia's profile. How could Sofia's father block the sale of the hotels the McNeills wanted if they were blameless in this matchmaking snafu?

But hiring an investigator served a second purpose, too—protecting Sofia's privacy.

Rising to his feet in one fluid motion, Cameron picked up his hard hat and shoved it onto his head.

"It makes sense to figure out what happened with Sofia's personal information before you move forward with your engagement." Cam checked his phone and put it in his pocket. "Or your wedding."

"Whoa." Quinn clapped a hand on his brother's back. Hard. "We're not getting married, as you damn well know."

The thought of spending a night with her revved him up fast, though. He didn't need that image in his head when he was on his way to meet her and talk through a plan for their fake engagement.

Then again, it wasn't as if he'd promised to keep his hands off her or anything. And she wanted the engagement to be believable. Already he was giving himself permission to get closer to her.

Much, much closer.

"You keep on telling yourself there's nothing going on." Cam shook off his hand and stalked toward the stairwell. "But no matter how much you play it off like Gramps' will doesn't matter to you, I know it's got to be in the back of your mind that you need to get married." Cameron rested a hand on the brick half wall that housed the stairs and faced Quinn. "Soon."

A dark expression clouded Cameron's features as he turned away, his steps echoing in the sudden silence as the jackhammer stopped. Quinn watched his brother walk away before he could argue. He was not getting married for the sake of McNeill Resorts, damn it. He was just running some damage control for the family business after his brother had made such a damn mess of things.

But maybe Cameron had a point. Quinn was attracted to her. He had to pretend to be her fiancé. There was no reason in the world he couldn't use this time to get closer to Sofia.

To enjoy Sofia.

To find out if that kiss had been a fluke or if the heat between them was every bit as scorching as he imagined.

Five

Sofia braided her wet hair in the large, shared dressing room after her shower, unwilling to attend her meeting with Quinn while drenched in sweat from her second class of the day. The writer Anton Chekov had once famously said that he knew nothing about the ballet but that the ballerinas "stink like horses" during the intervals, and the man had a point.

Digging in her bag for a hair tie, she scuttled past some of the junior dancers before she dropped into a chair near one of the makeup mirrors. The afternoon classes tended to have more of the sixteen- to eighteen-year-olds who could give her a run for her money physically, which had been just what she'd needed. After a day in the air yesterday, her body had felt off during her first class of the morning. So after her show rehearsals, she'd joined an afternoon session as well to will her body back into show shape. A day missed, and a dancer noticed. Besides, cramming every second of her day with hard work meant there were less opportunities for her older colleagues to quiz her about yesterday.

Or the huge rock on her finger.

She hadn't left the breathtaking ring on for long, but she'd worn it from the cab to the dressing room before removing it for dancing, causing a room full of whispers and raised eyebrows before the dancing master put everyone to work. She retrieved Quinn's gift now that she was in street clothes and slid the beautiful piece onto her finger. The few junior ballerinas remaining at the end of the day were in a heated discussion about the romantic availability of one of the male dancers.

"Holy crap, honey, look at that thing." Jasmine Jackson's voice surprised her, even though she should have been expecting her friend and publicist to meet her backstage for a quick meeting.

Jasmine rushed toward her, the heavy exit door banging shut behind her as she wove around stored stage lights and rolling racks of costumes covered in plastic. Petite with glossy hair so black it looked blue in certain light, Jasmine had attended ballet school with her in North Carolina for a year before Sofia's mother had caught the travel bug to tour Europe. Jasmine had quit dancing at thirteen with the arrival of hormones and serious curves. Many women would envy her figure, but Sofia had taken the phone calls from her distraught friend when her breasts had moved well into C-cup range—one of many physical changes that made dancing more difficult and casting directors overlook her. She'd been devastated.

Jasmine had ended up attending Syracuse University for communications and went on to work in advertising and promotions for the fitness industry. Her job paid well and brought her to New York, much to Sofia's delight. They'd shared an apartment for two years before Jasmine's budget had seriously outstripped hers and her friend had upgraded to a bigger place.

Sofia squeezed her hand in a fist to keep the ring in place. "I know. I'm terrified of losing it. And it seems really weird that it fits me, doesn't it?" Had her father shared such personal details with the matchmaker he'd hired? She had considered speaking to him today to assess how much her privacy had been breached. But she was still so angry with him over his presumptuous matchmaking tactics.

Jasmine bent to lift and examine Sofia's hand. A strand of silky black hair trailed over Sofia's wrist as her friend peered at the ring in the lights of the makeup mirror. As always, Jasmine looked so put together—her knee-length, gray-and-taupe sweater dress was formfitting underneath a tailored swing coat she left open. Bracelets clinked as she moved, everything about her girly and feminine. By contrast Sofia sported leggings and a man's dress shirt left untucked, with a black blazer—kind of her go-to work outfit in the colder months. With her wet hair braided, she felt more than a little dull next to glamorous Jasmine.

"Wow. Those diamonds are the real deal." Her Southern accent had softened over the years, but the lilt was still there. "Come on. Let's walk and talk so I can bring you up to speed before we meet with your very sexy fiancé."

Leave it to Jasmine to maintain the façade of this fake engagement in public. She was great at her job and a great friend, too. Jasmine had tried refusing payment for the work she did to promote Sofia's career, but she wouldn't hear of it. As it was, she knew the rate Jasmine gave her was far less than what her friend billed her corporate accounts.

"You're going into the coffee shop with me?" Sofia led the way out of the building, taking the less conspicuous path over West Sixty-Fifth Street instead of cutting through Lincoln Center. "I've been second-guessing myself and nervous about seeing him all day." She squeezed Jasmine's arm like a lifeline, grateful for a true friend after the past weeks of being on her guard at all times.

"Well, I hadn't planned on it." Jasmine frowned, oblivious to the male heads she turned as they navigated streets getting busier as rush hour neared. "The two of you have a lot to figure out."

"I know. But you're a major part of that." If Jasmine was there, it was like a business meeting—a way to coordinate schedules.

"Since when do you need a babysitter for a date? I'll say hello, but then I've got to go. I have an appointment downtown for happy hour drinks." Her work in PR happened over dinner and cocktails as often as it happened in a boardroom. "So fill me in on what happened today."

"Not much, thankfully." She'd been pleased with her plan to avoid talking about the engagement by outworking everyone in the room. "The only one who really cornered me about it was the ballet mistress, and she just warned me to remember that Idris Fortier would surely prefer any woman he worked with to devote one thousand percent to his ballet."

"Did you tell her that one thousand percent was a bit much?"

"Would I still have a job right now if I did?" The lighthearted moment ended quickly as Joe Coffee came into view and Sofia thought about seeing Quinn again.

Had she overestimated his appeal last night in her trancelike jet lag? She hoped so.

"How are your knees?" Jasmine asked. It was the only question that could rattle her more than Quinn.

Prone to knee problems, Sofia had injuries the same way all dancers had injuries. That is, always. Ballet was hard on the body and a dancer never knew when her time might be up. She feared for the length of her career, especially when she remembered the devil's bargain she'd made with her father as a teen. Two months after her mother died, he'd refused to let Sofia pursue a dance opportunity in St. Petersburg, insisting she finish her education in the US.

But after weeks of begging and crying—it was what her mother had wanted for her—he'd offered her a trade. She could go to Russia for dance school, but only if she promised that when her dance career was finished, she would come to work for him.

Which was not happening. He couldn't hold her to a deal she'd made as a teen. But she worried for her future with no backup plan after dance. Saying no to him when she had no prospects would be difficult. Staying in this expensive city would be virtually impossible. She willed away the ache in her knee and vowed to ice it longer tonight. It'd have to do.

"I had some twinges in my right knee in Kiev, but nothing that kept me off the stage." She tucked her shoulder bag closer as a family with two strollers pulled up beside them on the crosswalk. Horns and squeaky brakes mingled with the occasional sound of a doorman whistling for a cab in a cacophony her ears welcomed after six hours of Tchaikovsky and Stravinsky.

"Don't overdo it," Jasmine warned. "Staying healthy is more important than Idris and his ballet, no matter what you think."

"On the contrary, Idris and his ballet are my ticket to a post-dance career." She knew that a starring role and working closely with the superstar choreographer would completely change her profile in the dance world. It would open doors for a creative project she had in mind, but she needed someone like him to be on board. So she just had to nurse her knee through this opportunity.

Jasmine laughed. "You're the same as ever, Sofia. I think I could replay the conversations we had at nine and they'd be exactly the same ones we have today. You've always had a plan, I'll give you that."

Sofia slowed her step outside the door of Joe Coffee, grabbing Jasmine's arm.

"Not with Quinn McNeill, I don't." She wasn't intimidated by him or his money. Yet there was something about the way he made her feel that kept her anxious. Was it just physical attraction? Or did that anxiety mean something more worrisome?

Was it her gut telling her he was untrustworthy?

A messenger on a bicycle slammed his bike into the rack near them before entering the coffeehouse. The scent of fragrant Arabica beans and baked goods drifted through the door in his wake. Hunger reverberated in Sofia's stomach. Her diet was controlled and disciplined. Most days, she didn't mind. The sacrifice of cheesy fries and pizza had yet to outweigh the worth of her dream. But the smell of food tempted her so.

"He's just a man. The same as any other." Jasmine pursed her lips. "Your everyday average billionaire." She linked her arm through Sofia's and tugged her ahead. "Come on. I've got a few details to go over before I head out."

Squaring her shoulders, Sofia headed inside, determined not to let Quinn see that he made her uneasy. Distracted.

And far too interested in the attraction she'd felt for him the first moment their gazes had connected.

* * *

Head high, Sofia Koslov strolled into the coffee shop like a dancer and Quinn took notice from his seat at a table in the back corner. She carried herself differently than other women, a fact he'd picked up on yesterday before Cameron had proposed to her.

At that time he hadn't known what it was about her perfect posture and her graceful movements. Now he recognized it as her dance training that made her move like that. He couldn't picture her ever playing the Sugar Plum Fairy, however, despite the news clippings.

The Black Swan in *Swan Lake* maybe. She had a regal elegance, a sophistication. Her hair was pulled back into a damp braid that highlighted the long neck traditional in ballerinas. Her clothing was simple and understated so that the only thing that shone was the woman herself. And the ring on her left hand, he amended with satisfaction. Even staring at her across a crowded coffee shop, Quinn wanted her.

Damn.

He rose to greet the two women as they made their way through milling patrons juggling cups and cell phones. Her friend continued to shadow her step for step, a fact that disappointed him since he'd been eager to speak to Sofia privately. Or as privately as he could in a Manhattan java shop. He would have lobbied to meet at his apartment or in a quiet restaurant, but Sofia had been tired and rattled last night when they'd made these plans and he had the impression she'd purposely chosen someplace more public.

"Sofia." He greeted her the way he would greet a woman he loved, sliding an arm around her waist and kissing her cheek, mindful of the public atmosphere but still appropriately warm. He thought it better to be cautious since he didn't know her friend and wanted to be sure he played the part of Sofia's husband-to-be at all times.

Besides, it felt good to touch her.

The cool skin of her cheek warmed as his lips lingered for a moment. When he backed away, he spied the hint of color in her face before he extended a hand to her friend.

"Quinn McNeill," he introduced himself.

"Jasmine Jackson. I'm the best friend as well as the publicist. And total keeper of all her secrets." Her grip was firm and professional, and her eyes made it clear she knew full well about their ruse. "Shall we have a seat so I can go over my suggestions for the two of you?"

"Of course. Right this way." He gestured toward the table he'd secured in the back. Jasmine went first, and he palmed the small of Sofia's back to guide her along. Having his hands on her again made him realize how much he'd looked forward to acting out the part of fiancé.

He claimed the seat beside Sofia while Jasmine took the spot across from them and set down the leather binder on the maple surface between them.

"I've made copies of my ideal social calendar for both of you." She slid matching papers their way.

"I've already sent Sofia the digital file so she can forward it to you, Quinn."

Taking in the extensive notes on dates and events, he was impressed. She had details about the status of their invitations, directions, suggested attire, a who's who list of people they should try to speak to at each event and potential spots for photo ops. Clearly, the woman had done her homework and she'd done it in a hurry.

"I see you know the New York social calendar," he remarked, wondering if his company's PR firm would do half as good of a job. "This is ambitious."

As Sofia's finger followed the lines of type, the diamond engagement ring caught the last of the pale winter sunlight. As impressive as the piece was, and he was glad she'd worn it, he felt a ridiculous urge to replace it with something of his own choosing.

He hoped that normal brotherly competitiveness accounted for that instinct and not some latent sentimental notions. No way would he let his grandfather's dictate to marry get to him. He had decided to use this time with Sofia as a way to enjoy their obvious attraction. Not romanticize it.

"As I said." Jasmine closed her binder and folded her manicured fingers on top of the leather. "This is simply a wish list that would serve several purposes at once for Sofia."

"You got in touch with *Dance* magazine to reschedule our interview?" Sofia asked, her finger now stalled on a line item toward the bottom of the page.

"Yes. I told them today was full for you but that

you could meet with them Friday night during the welcome reception for Idris Fortier." Jasmine reached across the table to point out the event listed at the top of the paper. "In the meantime, I promised to release your statement about yesterday's events to them first." Jasmine pulled another set of papers from the binder and passed them across the table. "Here's a tentative release. If you could make your changes and send the digital file back to me before seven tonight, I can get it to the reporters for a blog post spot they're holding for you."

Quinn scanned the release, approving of the minimal personal details it included.

"'When we met'?" Sofia read a highlighted yellow section aloud. "'When we fell in love'? Is that really necessary?" Her gray eyes darted his way then back to her friend.

"Those are two questions everyone will ask. Better to save yourself answering it twenty times over and put out the information up front that you want people to see." Jasmine gave Sofia's forearm an affectionate squeeze. "But I will let you two discuss that since I need to run to another appointment."

Secretly pleased to have Sofia all to himself, Quinn rose as Jasmine took her leave. Sofia neatly folded the papers and tucked them into the black leather satchel she carried.

"Maybe we could talk through the rest of this while we walk? The park is close by. I know I suggested this place, but I wasn't thinking about how noisy it would be."

"Good idea." He left the waitress a tip even though they hadn't ordered, then escorted Sofia out onto the street. With a hand on her hip, he could feel the tension vibrating through her. Stress? Nervousness? He had a tough time reading her. "I live on the other side of the park. We could at least head in that direction."

The traffic would be gridlocked soon anyhow and he knew the paths well enough on the southern end of Central Park.

"Sounds good." She seemed slightly more relaxed outdoors. "And I'm sorry if this situation is cutting into your time. I probably wasn't in the best frame of mind to make decisions yesterday."

"Attending these events will only benefit my business." He turned down West Sixty-Ninth Street toward the park, plucking her bag off her shoulder to carry it for her. Fake fiancé or not, she would be his top priority for the upcoming weeks. She didn't seem like the type of woman who allowed other people to take care of her. But from where Quinn stood, she was in need of some spoiling—something this media ruse might let him do for her. "I haven't done much networking in the last year and it always lifts the company profile."

He wanted her at ease. Enjoying herself. Hell, he wanted to get to know her better and this would be the perfect time. So the less she worried about inconveniencing him, the better.

"That's a generous way to look at the situation. Thank you."

"I wouldn't call it generous." He tipped his head up

to the skies as a few snowflakes began to fall. "Are you going to be warm enough for this?"

Her blazer was heavy but now that the sun was almost down, the temperature was hovering just below freezing.

"My cape is in my bag," she said, pointing to the satchel on his shoulder. He lifted his arm so she could rifle through it and pull out the same mohair garment she'd worn the day before.

"Let me." Drawing her to the quieter side of the street near the buildings, he took the cape and draped it over her shoulders, then turned her so he could fasten the two big buttons close to her neck. His eyes met hers and, for half a heartbeat, that same awareness from their kiss danced in the air between them.

"I can get them," she protested, trying to sidle away politely.

He held fast, hands lingering on the placket as the snowfall picked up speed, coating her shoulders.

"But the more comfortable we get with each other now, the easier it's going to be to fool everyone on Friday." He looked forward to it.

Very much.

Part of it had something to do with the way her heartbeat quickened at his touch. He could feel the quick thrum beneath his knuckles right through her layers of clothing. He wanted to kiss her again, to taste her rosy lips where a snowflake quickly melted. But instead, he reached for the wide hood of her cape and drew it over her head to keep the snow off.

"Then I will try to think of this day as a dress rehearsal." She sounded so damn serious.

That, combined with some of the things she'd shared with him the night before, reinforced his notion of her as highly driven. He admired her work ethic and her dedication to her career. He'd always been the type to pour himself into a work project, too. Duty and perseverance were the cornerstones of his approach to the world.

"In that case, we can't go wrong." Readjusting her bag on his shoulder, he pressed a light hand to the small of her back to guide her through a left on Central Park West and the quick right to get on the path that would take them toward his apartment. "From what I gleaned about you last night as I read up on your career, it sounds like you've succeeded at everything you've set out to accomplish."

Even with the hood pulled up, he could see the way she smiled.

"Either that or I have an excellent publicist."

That surprised a laugh out of him as they strode deeper into the park, which seemed a bit busier than usual, the fresh snow bringing out kids and kids-at-heart. They passed people walking dogs and packs of middle-school-aged children in uniforms, still wearing backpacks.

"Jasmine does seem determined to package your career—and you—in the best possible way."

"She's a good friend and an equally awesome public relations manager."

"And this reception she wants us to attend. That's

for the choreographer you mentioned who's putting together the new ballet." He'd read about the guy a good bit last night. "The media can't use enough superlatives about him gracing New York with his presence." It had been a bit much in Quinn's mind, but then, he was far from an expert.

"You have been doing your research." She rewarded him with an approving smile that renewed the urge to kiss her.

But he also liked finding out more about her that would help him get closer to her. He would wait.

"This is a dress rehearsal for me, too, Sofia." He watched a few kids try to shake a radio-controlled helicopter down from some tree limbs; they were attracting an audience. "I'm trying to get my part down."

"You're doing well. If you were one of my students, you'd be promoted to the next level."

"You teach?" He paused on the outskirts of the crowd.

"A lot of the dancers do." Sofia's gaze went up to the helicopter and the kids shaking any branches of the old oak they could reach. "It's a way to pick up some extra income and give back to the company. The School of American Ballet is like our farm system… it feeds the City Ballet."

"Give me one second." He hated to interrupt her, but he also couldn't let the kids kill a tree that—for all he knew—could predate the damn park itself. He set down Sofia's bag and grabbed a football at one of the boys' feet as he strode into the group. "Guys, back up a minute."

The group did as he asked, a few calling out taunts that he'd never be able to reach the branch where the helicopter teetered. Which he welcomed, of course, since the ribbing only ensured that he'd throw twice as hard. He'd grown up with brothers, after all. He spoke the language.

"I get three shots," he insisted. "Only because I haven't warmed up my arm."

"I'll give you six, old man," shouted a wiry redhead who seemed to be the ringleader. "That thing is straight-up stuck."

Old?

Quinn told himself that he was only interested in saving the tree, but with a beautiful woman he wanted to impress watching from the sidelines, there was a chance he was fueled by another motivation altogether. Far from old…he was acting like a damn kid.

Backing up a step to adjust his aim, he cocked his arm and let the football fly.

Like in an ESPN highlight reel, the thing connected with the toy helicopter on the first try, earning cheers of admiration. And, because it had been so high up, the kids had time to run underneath the tree where the mouthy redhead caught it, scoring some of the victory for himself.

"Sorry about that." Quinn jogged back to Sofia, who stood on the path under a halo of light from a cast-iron street lamp. He grabbed her bag and hitched it higher on his shoulder.

With her hooded cape and the snow falling all around her, she looked like some exotic character from one of her ballets. A Russian princess, maybe.

"You appeared to have performed that trick a few times before," she observed.

"With two brothers? Of course. We got plenty of things caught in trees as kids. Kites were the worst to get down. By comparison, the helicopter was a piece of cake." His warm breath lingered in the cool air, making it seem as though his words hung in the space between them. A gust of wind sent a slight chill through him. Glancing at Sofia, he noticed her hair was still wet.

"I can't imagine what it would be like to have siblings." The loneliness in her words was evident.

"Your bio doesn't say much about your family." He knew because he'd scoured it for details about her.

"In the past, I tried to keep my personal life and work life separate. Not that I have a lot of personal life to speak about." She stared up at Tavern on the Green as they passed. The restaurant looked sort of otherworldly in the snowfall with the trees and white lights all around. "But my mother died when I was thirteen and I am not close with my father."

"I'm sorry about your mother." He took her hand for the dash across West Drive before they reached quieter roads through the middle of the park. "That must have been a really difficult age to lose a parent."

He didn't let go of her hand since her fingers were chilled. And because he wanted to touch her. Besides, they would be in the public eye again soon enough, where they would have to sell themselves as a loving couple.

As if she understood his motivations, she leaned into him and the spicy smell of her currant perfume wafted up to him. Hooking her arm through his, she drew closer.

"I was devastated. All the more so because my mother hated my father, which meant I hated him, too. Then, suddenly, after her death I was left with him." Sofia pushed off her hood as they reached denser growth that limited how much snow fell on them. Maybe she'd just been looking for a reason to untwine their fingers. "To this day, I don't know what drew the two of them together since he represented everything she despised. She called the privileged wealthy a 'soulless culture.'"

"What about you?" Quinn wondered where that left him in her world view. "Do you agree with your mother?"

"Wait." She turned around to look at the path they'd just traveled, tugging on his arm so they stood off the walkway to one side. "Let's stop for a second and take it in."

She didn't have to explain what she meant. This part of the park was beautiful on any given day. But in a fresh snowfall, with the Tavern on the Green glowing from within and the tree trunks and branches draped in white lights, the view was like no other in the city. The snow dulled the sounds from the streets nearby, quieting rush hour to white noise.

Standing with Sofia at his side made it all the more appealing. The glow of the white lights reflected on her face.

"Beautiful." His assessment, while simple, was heartfelt.

"But you know what my mother taught me about beauty?" Sofia asked, a mischievous light in her liquid silver eyes. "It is not a matter of just looking beautiful. It should surround us." She held her hand out, palm up to catch snowflakes. "Feel special." Inhaling deeply, she smiled with her eyes closed. "Have a unique scent when you breathe it in. And if you can catch it on your tongue, the taste will be beautiful, too."

He watched, transfixed, as this aloof and disciplined dancer stuck her tongue out and tipped her head to the sky.

Another time, he might have laughed at her antics. But she seemed lost in a happy childhood memory, and he didn't want to spoil it. Reaching for her hand full of snowflakes, he warmed her palm with his and peered upward through the white branches at the hint of stars beyond.

"You're right." He felt the beauty around him, that much was certain. But it had more to do with the slide of her damp fingers between his. With the tattoo of the pulse at her wrist that he felt on his palm.

"Did you catch one?" She lowered her chin to meet his gaze, her eyes still alight with a glow of happiness.

But she must have seen another expression reflected in his face because her smile faded.

"No." He reached for her jaw to thumb a snowflake

from her creamy cheek, her skin impossibly soft to
the touch. Capturing her chin in his hand, he angled
her lips for a taste. "But I'm about to."

Six

Transported by the snow, the city and the man, Sofia hadn't been expecting the kiss, and maybe it was her total lack of defenses that let her feel the pleasure of it. She delighted in the warm pressure of his mouth in contrast to such a cold day. The soft abrasion of his chin where the new of growth of whiskers rubbed over her tender skin oversensitive from the wind. The gentle way he touched her face to steer her where he wanted, to better delve between her lips.

Answering his demand by stepping closer, craving the warmth of the man, Sofia lost herself.

Quinn's kiss was the second act of *Swan Lake*. Or maybe *Giselle*. Or maybe it was every romantic moment she'd ever danced and never felt deeply until this moment. She squeezed his hand where he'd entwined their fingers, enjoying the way her body fit against him. They weren't like two dancers with bodies that complemented one another. But like a man possessing a woman, lending her his strength so she didn't have to draw from her own.

It was a moment of heaven.

When he slowly pulled away from her and she felt the snowflakes fall on her skin again now that he did not completely shelter her, the cool ping of the tiny drops urged her out of her romantic swoon. And no doubt about it, she stood in Central Park swooning on her feet for a man she'd met the day before.

"Quinn, we have a lot of work we should be doing." She blurted the words with no segue and zero grace. "If we want to get that press release out on time, that is."

Untangling her fingers from his, she brushed by him to continue walking...east? Her brain scrambled to regain thought. Yes, east. What on earth had gotten into her? Had that kiss been part of the role he seemed determined to play for her? Or had he truly felt inspired to kiss her?

"You're right." Quinn didn't need to walk fast to keep up with her as she practically jogged through the park. His longer strides ate up the ground easily. As he glanced at her, the light reflected devilishly in his eyes. "But I want you to know I liked kissing you, Sofia. Very much. There's no reason we shouldn't enjoy ourselves over the next few weeks."

Sharp, cold air entered her lungs. "Just because we are within easy reach doesn't mean we should automatically start touching." She didn't want to be a convenient outlet for him. "But what's our story for how we met or when we met?"

"I was introduced to your father at the Met Gala. Were you there with him?"

"Of course not. Do you have any idea what a ticket costs to that event?" At moments like this she could understand how her mother might have come to believe the wealthy were living in a different universe from regular people. The Met Gala was so far beyond her price range it was laughable.

"Actually, no." He stuffed his hands into the pockets of his overcoat, his profile in shadow as they walked. "I was on the guest list because I made a donation to the museum."

Right. Which meant he'd paid more than the ticket price that was almost half her annual salary. Like her father, Quinn belonged to a world of wealth and unreality. A world she had purposely avoided.

"Suffice it to say, we didn't meet there." She wished she'd worn warmer clothes for their walk. Her knees were feeling the effects of the cold.

"What if we say we met here? In the park? We bonded over rescuing a kid's toy stuck in a tree last spring." As a bicyclist churned through the growing snow cover, Quinn slid a protective arm around her, his hand an enticing warmth through her cape before his touch fell away again. "At least we don't have to make up something fictional. We base it on today, but say it happened when I was walking home one evening and you were taking a break in the park."

"That could work." She nodded, locking down the time frame in her mind and trying to envision today's scene in a different season. "Although I would never give a stranger I met in the park my contact information."

"Maybe I started taking that route home every day, hoping to see you. Two weeks later, bingo. There you were again. We fell in love over the next few months, and that should be all we need to fill out Jasmine's press release." He slowed as they passed Central Park Zoo and headed toward Fifth Avenue. "Are you all right?"

"Of course," she answered automatically. "Why?"

"You're limping."

"No I'm not." She couldn't be. Refused to be. She excelled at hiding injuries on stage. Perhaps she just didn't give much thought to her gait in her private time. "Just hurrying to get home."

She couldn't read his expression in the dark.

"I should have insisted on a car. We're almost there."

"I'm fine. And if you can point me to the closest subway station? I thought there was one on Fifth?"

"Come inside and warm up first. I'll drive you home."

"That's not necessary. As you pointed out, we have enough for the press release. I'll send it over to Jasmine when I get home."

"We haven't firmed up plans for the Fortier reception." As they emerged from the park, he crossed Fifth Avenue at East Sixty-First. "Besides, my building is right here. I can send out that release for you, and I'll call you a car afterward." He stopped outside the Pierre.

He lived in the hotel?

Of course he did. It was a gracious, old New York address with five-star service. The small part of her that was still her father's daughter could already envision the kind of food room service provided here.

"Sofia." Quinn lowered his voice as they stood under the awning in front of the building. "We're committed to this course now. Let's be sure we deliver a believable performance."

"Believable because we show up for all of those public appearances as a couple?" She lowered her voice even more in deference to the doorman who was pulling open a cab door for a newcomer. "Or believable because we're kissing in our spare time?"

Quinn seemed to weigh the idea carefully. "If you truly think that the kiss was a bad idea, we'll make sure all future displays of affection are strictly for show and limit them to the public sphere."

She wasn't sure if she was disappointed or relieved. Maybe a little of both.

"That might help." At least then she'd be prepared before he kissed her again. She'd have her guard up. Her body would receive a warning before he stoked it to life with a mere flick of his tongue. "Thank you."

"Will you come inside, then? We can have dinner sent up while we fill in the blanks for Jasmine and send out the statement." Quinn had been both patient and reasonable.

Of course, he was only doing any of this for the sake of his business concerns, protecting the McNeill interests from the threats her father had made at the airport last night. She needed to remember that, even if his kisses told a different story. Quinn was simply more experienced. Worldly. Maybe even jaded. Some people could kiss solely for passion's sake, not love, but she'd never been that kind of woman.

Or so she thought. Maybe she'd just never met a man she could truly feel passionate about? Unlike her friends, she'd never been a boy-crazy teenager. Her attention and love had always belonged to the stage.

"Okay," she agreed, the chill in her bones making the decision for her, damn it. Or maybe it was the promise of something more delicious than the banana and crackers that awaited her at home.

It wasn't Quinn's fault she was far more attracted to him than she'd ever been to any man. Deep in thought as they entered the hotel, they rode a private, key-operated elevator to his floor. Even the elevator was opulent, inlaid with gold, and the deep rich scarlet carpet showed no signs of wear. The doors swished opened into a large foyer and a view through the living room to Central Park.

The apartment took up an entire floor.

She should have guessed from the engagement ring she still wore that he would live this way. His family owned a resort chain, while he himself managed a hedge fund. Exactly the kind of man she would have never envisioned herself with. But in spite of the multimillion-dollar views, his apartment was decorated with tasteful restraint. Coffee-toned walls were a warm backdrop for sleek, gray furnishings punctuated with some rust-colored accents—a vase, matched roman shades that covered the top third of the huge windows. Comfortable and attractive, the room pulled her forward as Quinn switched on the fireplace and put in a call to the hotel's kitchen.

An hour later, picking over the remains of her chicken fricassee while seated on a giant leather couch that wrapped around a corner of Quinn's apartment, Sofia had to admit she felt glad to be there. The snow had stopped outside the living room windows, but peering down into the park with all the street lamps lit was sort of like looking into a dollhouse with hundreds of different tiny rooms. He was putting the finishing touches on the press release on his laptop. A fire crackled in the fireplace, warming her feet and knees, and she'd even accepted a throw blanket made of the softest cashmere ever.

With silent apologies to her mother, Sofia decided that no one truly soulless would help a scrappy thirteen-year-old retrieve a toy. Or help Sofia carry off a mad scheme to pretend to have a fiancé. Quinn was an exception to her mother's rule about rich people.

"Just confirming...when did we know we were in love?" Quinn had taken the easy chair diagonally across from her, maintaining a professional amount of space between them.

"How about when you ordered the chicken fricassee for me?" she offered, trying to stick to the truth the way he'd showed her earlier.

"No one could blame you for being wooed by the food here." He quit typing and peered over at her in the firelight.

They hadn't put any other lights on in this room, although there was a glow from the kitchen. Sofia had been enjoying looking outside and the view was easier to appreciate with less light behind her.

"Dancers are perpetually starving," she admitted. "So I'm more susceptible than most to good food."

"Why are you always starving?" Quinn set aside the laptop long enough to clear their plates and set the dishes on a serving cart that had been delivered half an hour ago.

"It's a figure of speech. I expend a great deal of energy, for one thing. And, for another, the body preferred by most directors is very slender."

The topic had come under more debate over the last few years with a move to recognize healthy bodies of all sizes in dance. But ballet was rooted in traditions on every level, and she didn't know any company that truly embraced this philosophy yet.

"I'm surprised. I would think the moves require a great deal of strength."

"They do. But we need to build that strength in different ways. Repetition of lighter weights, for example."

"But why?" He took the seat closer to her now, sharing the couch even though he was a couple feet away. He'd brought his laptop with him but hadn't opened it yet.

"Choreographers like a company of dancers that

are all roughly the same size and build. There's more symmetry to it when we all move."

"And you'd still get that if you all agree to be ten pounds heavier. And wouldn't more muscle minimize injury?"

"Yes and no. Some say a lighter frame puts less strain on the joints."

"You can't eat enough. You work constantly. You're subject to intra-squad jostling for position—so much so you're willing to fake an engagement to keep your detractors quiet." He counted off the negatives on his fingers. "So if you're willing to go through all that, I have to think there's one hell of an upside for you."

"There is." She shifted positions, straightening as she warmed to her subject. "I watched *Sleeping Beauty* with my mother as a child. It was a performance in the middle of nowhere—a tiny troupe traveling through Prague. And I was captivated by Aurora like any other little girl who attends the ballet." Sliding off the couch, she moved to an open spot on the floor to show him. "I thought the dancer was the most beautiful and elegant woman in the world." She took a position for the Rose Adagio dance in her stocking feet, imagining a princely suitor before her as she mimicked Aurora's questioning pose with one leg raised and curved behind her. "When she took the roses from each of her four suitors…" She mimed the action, having danced the role many times herself. "I knew I wanted to *be* her. Not just Aurora, but the dancer who brought her to life."

Quinn's blue gaze tracked the movement of her arched foot as she lifted it in the exaggerated extension that her Russian teachers had stressed. The warmth in his eyes—his attention to her body—did not inspire the same feelings as when she captured an audience's imagination on stage. This felt personal in a way that heated her skin and made her all too aware of her appearance.

Not just her body, which was perpetually displayed in dance. But the stroke of her braid against one arm. The rush of air past her lips as her breath caught.

"So you dance for the love of it. Because it was your dream." He kept the conversation focused, which she appreciated since she'd forgotten what they were talking about for a moment, distracted by the sparks that crackled between them.

"I have never wanted to do anything else." Which was why she feared the end of her career, a moment that could sneak up on her on any given night, with her body constantly battling injuries.

She needed to reach the top of her field now—as quickly as possible—to achieve the fame necessary to parlay the experience into success afterward. And she needed to dance the starring role for Fortier to make that happen.

"Ballet is your passion." Quinn let the word simmer between them for a long moment before returning his attention to the laptop. "And I think I know when we fell in love."

He began typing.

"You do?" Her heartbeat stuttered in her chest. She

forced herself to sit back down and resume normal conversation in spite of the nerve endings flickering to life all over her body.

Too late she realized she had sat closer to him than she'd been before. She told herself that was only so she could peer over his shoulder at whatever it was he was typing. She caught a hint of his male scent, something clean like soap or aftershave that made her want to breathe deeply.

"It was the first time I saw you dance." His fingers paused on the keyboard, the sudden quiet seeming to underscore the moment and stirring to life a whole host of complicated feelings.

His words should not affect her this way. Especially since they were spinning tall tales for the media and not discussing anything remotely real.

"Name the performance. I'll tell the whole world how your movements on the stage captured me. When I watched you dance, I saw how passion guides you and knew we were a match."

"You toy with me," she accused, scuttling back to her previous position on the couch. "Your words are like your kisses—all for show. But I find them confusing."

"I'm not toying with you." He passed her the laptop. "You should read this over."

How could she concentrate on the words when her blood ran too hot and she kept imagining the way his eyes had followed her body while she danced?

"I'm sure it's fine." She set the laptop on the couch

between them. "Jasmine will review it before she sends it out."

"Sofia?" He moved the laptop to the coffee table, edging closer. "I don't know how else to approach this to make you more comfortable. But *you* wanted to put on this show. I'm trying to help you."

His voice, deep and masculine, sent a shiver through her.

"Thank you. But I would prefer if this remained a performance for the benefit of others. I don't want to play at the game when we are alone." She felt his nearness in the same way that she knew without looking where her dance partner would be at all times. Except that was practiced, a trick she'd learned through study and repetition. With Quinn, her cells seemed to seek out his presence, attuning themselves to him without her even thinking about it.

"The only reason I kissed you in the park is because I'm attracted to you. I won't pretend otherwise." With a shuddering breath, his eyes, which a moment ago blazed with heat, seemed to ember as his voice lilted with resignation. "But I can put a rein on that, and I have."

"How? How do you put a rein on it, as you say?" She wondered if he had tricks of his own. Something she might learn for herself.

"It's not easy. And it gets tougher the longer I'm with you." He lifted his hand toward her face the way he'd done in the snowfall right before he'd kissed her. But then he lowered his fingers again, hand falling to his side. "We have an agreement, however, and

I'll do what it takes to see it through. If that means we play this your way, I'm going to do everything in my power to keep my hands to myself unless we're in public."

"The way we will be on Friday." At the reception for Idris Fortier. Her first real public appearance with Quinn as a couple, and it would be a major moment in her career.

Butterflies fluttered through her belly at the thought of being on this man's arm all evening. Feeling his hand at her waist or grazing her hip through a thin evening gown.

Pretending to be in love.

Her lips tingled as she wondered if he would kiss her.

"Yes." His gaze dipped to her mouth as if he could read her mind. "I'm already looking forward to it."

Seven

Tossing generous handfuls of Epsom salt into the tub, Sofia ran the hot water, anticipating the effects of the bath. Her muscles ached and it was only Wednesday.

As she let the water fill the tub, she pumped toning soap onto her hands and then her face, before splashing water from the faucet to wash away a day of sweat and stress. A candle flickered on the sink's countertop, sending a soothing scent of lavender into the air. When she was a small girl, her mother would always burn lavender candles after a long day. Although only a small connection to life before her mom passed away, the fragrance still relaxed her.

And she needed that now more than ever.

Deep breath in. Deep breath out.

Washing the rest of the soap from her face, Sofia tried to focus on preparing for the private audition for Idris Fortier in less than a week. That should be her sole thought.

But instead thoughts of Quinn pushed into her head. It had been two nights since they'd walked through the park and a day since her interview with *Dance* magazine where she'd relayed the love story she and Quinn had manufactured. The details seemed all too real. And she kept replaying their brief time together. His lips, his touch. How she was attracted to him, though she knew better.

Even after her bath, she was frustrated as hell. She stepped out of the tub, water dripping from her body onto a bath mat, and tested her knee carefully. And, thank heaven, it held. It felt better if not perfect. She shrugged on a short, fluffy bathrobe and yanked the tie into a knot.

Patting her face dry with a semi-plush hand towel, she examined her reflection in the mirror. She could do this. She could nail the audition and be the star that Idris Fortier wanted for his next ballet. That connection would do so much for her. Give her career legs after her physical ones quit giving her the lift and height she needed on her jumps.

Stashed on the corner of the countertop was a collection of reviews from the most reputable critics about Fortier's last ballet. Jasmine had sent this particular stack over to her apartment. When Sofia had an audition on her radar, she always poured over press releases and reviews, trying to glean a better sense of her audience.

Sifting through the documents once more, a headline caught her eye.

Affair.

She eased herself down onto the edge of the tub and put her feet back in the water as she devoured the article. Apparently the choreographer had had an affair with the star of his last production. The weight of that information unsettled her.

Her phone chirped, startling her. Pulling it out of the pocket of her robe, she glanced at the screen.

Quinn.

"Hello." Heart fluttering, she felt a mixture of excitement and nerves crash in her chest.

"Hello, Sofia." His voice incited a flush of warmth over her skin beneath the robe.

"Quinn." His name felt like an endearment on her tongue. "Hello," she said again. To cover her surprise.

She closed her eyes and saw him there—with her—in the tub. Her mouth went dry.

"I thought you might like an update about the matchmaker situation," he continued.

Something that felt an awful lot like disappointment pounded in tandem with her heartbeat. Had she really just wanted him to call for no reason? If this faux engagement was going to work, she'd have to keep her emotions in check.

"Of course. Tell me." The news clipping about Idris's affair was still in her hand; she stared at it while

Quinn's baritone voice filled the speaker, willing her pulse back to normal.

She hadn't called her father since announcing her engagement at the airport, despite how angry she'd been with him at the time. That night, she'd been too exhausted to do battle with him, and Quinn had told her he would take care of making sure her dating profile was removed from wherever it had been posted.

"I'm not sure if I mentioned that Cameron's matchmaker is Mallory West. He contacted her for an explanation the day after he proposed to you."

The name meant nothing to Sofia, but as her dancing peers had noted, she wasn't part of the Manhattan singles scene.

"Did she say where she got my flight information?" She had thought about that more than once. How could Cameron's matchmaker have known her arrival time in New York, while her father claimed to be ignorant of Cam's appointment to meet her?

She dipped her hand into the bubbles in the tub, skimming her fingers across the soapy tops.

"She told Cameron she would look into it." Quinn's voice was as potent as his touch. If she closed her eyes, she could imagine him beside her. "But since then, her phone has been disconnected and her email generates an autoreply that she's out of the country on an extended trip."

Sofia forced her eyes open, thinking about that bit of peculiar news. Her cheeks puffed with a hefty exhale. "What do you think it means?"

"For now, it simply means that she is a dead end in

our hunt for information. I'm sorry, Sofia. But I will continue having my IT technician hunt for any sign of her online. And, for what it's worth, he's seen no traces of a dating profile for you online, so I think the matchmaker your father hired made good on her promise to pull it down."

"At least that part is good news." She really needed to call her father and ask him more about the situation herself, if only to find out whom he'd hired to help her with her dating prospects. She would feel better once she told that person in no uncertain terms that she wasn't interested.

"It is. And we'll figure out the rest of it, Sofia," Quinn assured her before his tone shifted and his voice got lower. "But that isn't the only thing we have to figure out."

"No?" Sensations tripped down her spine at that sexy rasp in his voice. "What else should we be discussing?"

A half laugh sounded from the other end of the call and nothing else, no background noise, just him. He must be somewhere private. Alone. "Something more fun. So, Sofia, what kind of dress should I buy you to wow and woo the crowds at Idris Fortier's reception on Friday? Do you have a favorite boutique?"

Buy her a dress? The gesture was sweet. But it was too much. Far too much.

"That is kind of you, but definitely not necessary." Still, she imagined what he would choose for her. What it would be like to slide on a garment hand-picked by Quinn?

"I'll take you shopping anywhere you'd like."

She tried not to think about the beautiful things a man like Quinn McNeill could afford.

"You are thoughtful, Quinn, but I can't accept more gifts." She felt guilty enough about wearing that massive diamond on her left hand, but he'd convinced her the ring was a necessity. "And I already have something in mind." She didn't mean for her voice to sound so clipped.

"Are you nervous?" he pressed, the deep tones of his whiskey-rich voice warming her moist body.

Her instincts kicked in; she could tell he was interested. He actually wanted to know.

"A bit. I… I just…" Her voice trailed off. Social gatherings and big parties were not her thing. She disliked superficial small talk, preferring meatier conversations.

Music.

Dancing.

"Yes?" he prompted.

"I'm terrible at galas. And around large masses of humanity in general."

"Seriously?" Surprise colored his voice. "But you dance in front of large audiences."

"Yes, seriously. I have stage fright in social scenarios where I'm forced to talk. But when I'm on stage, ballet feels like poetry, like breath. It's different. Completely different." Chewing her lip, she felt a ball of anxiety begin to form.

Deep breath.

"Luckily for you, I'm quite the pro at these galas.

I'll be there to guide and help you, if you want to follow my lead, that is."

"If you can speak in coherent sentences, you'll be one step ahead of me. I'm notoriously awkward in interviews. Jasmine has tried to coach me, but I get very tense."

"I hope that having me there helps. But either way, we'll get through it. And if you want to leave early, I'll give everyone the impression that it's my fault because I can't wait to have you all to myself."

The images that came to mind heated her skin all over again. So much so, she needed to pull her feet out of the hot water.

"How generous of you," she observed, feeling tongue-tied already but for a very different reason.

"I do what I can." The smile in his voice came right through the call. "So can I ask what you plan on wearing?"

A playful tone from him? Now, wasn't that a surprise. Smiling, she glanced out of the bathroom and into her bedroom, eyeing her closet where she had exactly nothing appropriate.

While her father would have loved to write her monthly checks or set up a trust fund for his sole heir, she'd resisted all of his efforts to share his wealth with her in any way. Her mother had always blamed him for his refusal to focus on the things that really mattered in life. Like love. Family. Art. All the things that mattered most to Sofia.

She would do without a dress.

"Something stunning," she told Quinn finally,

wondering if she could get something on loan from the costume department.

"Something sexy?" He pressed and she heard his smile through the phone.

"Extremely," she said, forgetting that she was supposed to keep herself in check around him.

Chuckling, his voice was low like a whispered promise. "I look forward to seeing every sexy inch of you on Friday."

And before she could close her gaping jaw, he'd hung up.

Quinn stepped from the limo outside Sofia's apartment building shortly before seven on the night of the reception for her big-deal choreographer.

He hit the call button near the door and waited to be buzzed in before heading inside and taking the elevator to her floor. They'd spoken by phone the last two nights and their conversations had allowed him to get closer to Sofia without the in-person surge of attraction getting in the way. She seemed more at ease on the phone, as if she needed that cerebral connection before she'd allow herself to admit the physical chemistry that had been apparent to him since the first moment he'd seen her.

He'd even talked her into letting him send her a gown for tonight, a feat it had taken him a lot of effort to pull off. He'd only gotten his way by arguing that it would make their engagement more believable. He would absolutely want his fiancée to appear at such an important event for her career in an unforgettable, one-of-a-kind dress. Especially since this would be their first formal public outing as an engaged couple.

Now, as he rang the bell outside 5C, he mentally reviewed the game plan. *Let the attraction build. Don't rush her.* But once they were in the spotlight and she needed to sell their relationship as a stable, happy union that wouldn't detract from her dancing, he planned to deliver. She would be in his arms as often as possible to prove it.

And he looked forward to that more than he'd anticipated any date in a long time. So much for the idea that all this was for show or to smooth over relations with her father. Quinn wasn't going through with it just to ease those European deals and to save his brother from embarrassment.

When the door opened, the sight of her hit him in his chest like a physical blow. Not because she was beautifully dressed, although she damn well looked incredible in her navy-silk gown with subtle, breezy feathers covering much of the skirt to the floor-length hem, her blond hair artfully arranged so it was half up and half down, the tendrils snaking along her neck. He would have been affected if she'd been in a T-shirt and shorts.

He'd missed her. And that realization rocked him.

"You look incredible, Sofia." She looked like the woman he wanted more than any other. Her wide, smoke-colored eyes picked up hints of silver when she wore navy. Diamond roses glittered in her ears.

"You clean up rather nicely yourself." She reached to touch him, surprising the hell out of him in the best possible way, but in the end she merely rubbed the fabric of his tuxedo sleeve appreciatively. "That's a gorgeous tux."

"Thanks," he answered absently, his mind on stun at a simple brush of her fingers. He wanted her touching all the rest of him that way. But he breathed deep and stuck to the game plan.

"Are you ready to go?" He stepped inside her apartment, following her while she retrieved a beaded purse.

"Almost. I couldn't get the hook at the top." She presented him with her back. A soft scent like vanilla mingled with musk drifted up from her hair as he swept aside some of the blond tendrils to find the clasp.

What was it about the nape of a woman's neck that drove a man insane? The vulnerability of it? The trust in exposing it? Quinn wanted to lean closer and lick her there, kiss his way to the back of her ear and then down the column of her throat again.

He settled for taking his time with the clasp, his knuckles lightly brushing beneath the fabric of her dress. He felt the answering quiver in her body. They were that close. Sealing his eyes shut for a moment— needing to control his runaway thoughts—he finished the job and reached around her to take the evening wrap, settling it on her shoulders.

"Time to leave," he urged, wanting nothing so much as to get her in public so he could touch her. How backward was that? Most men couldn't wait to get a woman home to be alone. But he'd promised her their physical contact would be just for show. "Do you have a coat?"

Quinn needed a public audience as an excuse to put his hands on her.

But maybe tonight would change that. Make Sofia realize the effort of staying away from each other wasn't worth it when they could explore the heat between them to their thoroughly mutual satisfaction.

"A cape." She reached for a long black cape with fur around the oversize hood. Lovely. Elegant. Like her.

Before she could move further, he took it from her and draped it reverently over her shoulders. She looked like a timeless screen star in that movie *Doctor Zhivago*.

Damn, he was getting downright sentimental. He needed air. Bracing, cold air.

Leaving her apartment behind—thank God the elevator was crowded to keep him in check—he offered his arm and was glad she took it as they walked toward the vestibule. As a dancer used to working on her toes, she must be comfortable in the sky-high silver heels he glimpsed beneath the dress hem as she walked. But with damp spots on the hall floor from the snow tracked indoors, it helped that she could hold on to him for support.

Once they were inside the limo and headed uptown to the gala venue, Sofia placed a hand on her chest.

"Can I just tell you I'm a nervous wreck?"

"Just remember, you're a professional at the top of her career about to impress a choreographer who is probably already very eager to work with you." Quinn had read up on Idris Fortier over the course of the week, as well as the dance world's frenzied reaction to his New York arrival.

"You don't know that. Some of my reviews are solid." She spoke quickly, settling her purse beside her as they stopped at a red light. "But I have received plenty of harsh criticism, too, and I know my own shortcomings, so Fortier might decide—"

"I read your reviews, Sofia. They're more than solid." He wanted to halt her before she strayed too far down that road of what-ifs and worry. "Some say you favor technique over artistry, the sport of it over the dancing, and you don't trust your partners enough." He'd scoured the praise and the criticism in an effort to understand her more, to be closer to her. "But I compared your reviews to the rest of the stars in the company, and I don't see anyone who comes away more favorably. In fact, critics agree you are the most exciting talent to work here in years. If I can glean that as a novice, an insider like Fortier will be well aware of you."

"I'm not so sure about that." She wound one of the long, loose feathers of her skirt around her finger where the cape had fallen away. He noticed how her nails were polished a clear pink, and her engagement ring was practically glowing in the limo's dome lighting.

But her movements suggested she was more than a little nervous.

"May I make a suggestion?" He covered her hand

where she'd gently destroyed the single feather, breaking his own rule about not touching her in private.

"I don't suppose it could hurt." The tension in her body was so obvious she practically vibrated with it. "What is it?"

"Considering that you're visibly anxious about tonight..." he began. But before he could propose the idea, she made a small sound of distress. Uncrossing and re-crossing her legs in the opposite direction, her foot nudged his calf and then began to jitter.

"Oh, God." She swallowed hard. "I *will* get it together. Even though there is so much riding on making a good impression—"

"Listen. We make a good team. Remember how easily we ran off the journalists from *Dance* magazine at the airport? I know your goals tonight and I'm good at things like this. Follow my lead and you'll be fine." He twined his fingers through hers, hoping to impart some calm, not just because he wanted to touch her.

"You think I can after reading how I don't trust a partner?" she asked dryly. "I've gotten dropped on several occasions. It doesn't inspire confidence."

Sofia's forced smile and raised brow struck him. He needed to assure her that he wasn't one of those types of partners. He'd be there.

Pulling her gaze away from his, she stared out the window, eyes actively scanning the buildings and pedestrians on the sidewalk.

"I can imagine." He smoothed his thumb over the back of her hand, liking the feel of her skin and the way his touch relaxed her. He could sense some of the tension leaking away as her musky vanilla perfume seemed to invite him closer. "But I would never let you fall."

"Well. Thank you." Her gaze fell to their locked fingers, as if she were surprised to see the way they were connected. "I will admit that I could use a steadying presence tonight."

A car horn blared outside and a faint crescendo of sirens filled the air. Oh, New York.

"Good. Now, about my suggestion." He traced the outline of her engagement ring with his finger, extraordinarily aware of her calf still grazing his knee. "It might help if you allowed me to distract you."

"Distract me?" She arched an eyebrow at him, skeptical but no longer nervous. Her jittering foot came to a rest.

If anything, the sudden stillness of her body suggested she just might be intrigued.

"It's completely up to you." He wanted nothing so much as to gather her up and settle her on top of him. But he had a plan and he would take his time. Let her get used to the idea of enjoying every moment of their time together. "But we could rechannel all that nervous energy. Give it a different physical outlet."

Her jaw dropped.

"I am not the kind of woman who has sex in a limousine," she informed him, not looking quite as scandalized as she might have.

He, on the other hand, was plenty surprised her mind had gone there.

"Well, damn. That's an incredible thought, but I wasn't suggesting we take things that far. You look too beautiful to mess up before your big night, Sofia."

"Then be more clear," she snapped, her cheeks pink and her eyes alight with new fire. "Because I have no idea what you mean."

In a blink, he shifted positions, releasing her hand so he could bracket her shoulders between his arms, pinning her without touching her. He held her gaze, lowering himself closer until his chest came within inches of her breasts. Even with her dress and cape between them, he could see their gentle swell.

He spoke softly in her ear.

"Distraction." He articulated it clearly so there would be no mistake. "I could kiss you somewhere that wouldn't mess you up. A spot along the curve of your lovely neck, maybe." His eyes wandered over her, assessing the possibilities. "Or beneath your hair."

A shiver ran through her while his breath warmed the space between her skin and his mouth. Careful not to touch her, he let the idea take hold. If nothing else, he felt damn certain just this conversation would rewire her thoughts for a while, taking them off the choreographer she was so anxious to impress.

The notion satisfied him. A lot.

"That is a crazy idea," she whispered back. "Letting you kiss me might give me more heart palpitations than I was having before."

He wanted a taste of her. So. Badly.

"But the heart palpitations I could give you would be the pleasurable kind." Dragging his attention off the rapid pulse at her throat, he heard her quick intake of breath, saw her eyelids flutter once. Twice.

"You are way too sure of yourself, Quinn McNeill." Her hands lifted, hovering near his shoulders as if she debated touching him there.

He willed her palms closer.

"No. I'm sure of what's between us even though you don't want to acknowledge it."

"We're only pretending," she insisted, her eyebrows furrowing as the limo slowed to another stop, jostling her closer to him. She braced her palms on his chest. Torture. Pure torture.

He hoped their destination was another hour away because he was locking that limo door if anyone tried to open it now.

"I only agreed to pretend because I was attracted to you to start with." The words were out of his mouth. He couldn't take them back, and what surprised him was he didn't want to.

"What are you saying?" She shook her head, squinting as she tried to process. "Next month, this will be all over—"

"I know." Gently he edged her wrap back and smoothed aside a few locks of silky hair that curled around her neck and rested against the fur-lined hood. "But until then, I want this."

Pressing his lips to the curve of her shoulder, he soaked in the warmth and fragrance unique to this woman. Sweet and musky at the same time, her scent made him instantly hard. Not moving, he wanted to take his cue from her, only advancing this game as far as she'd let him.

When her hands finally landed on his shoulders, for a moment he thought she might push him away. Instead her fingers tunneled under his open coat, then farther inside his jacket, splaying out over his tuxedo shirt until he could feel the soft scrape of her short nails through the cotton.

The sensation raked over his senses, arousing a fierceness in him that had no place in a limo five minutes before a party. He opened his mouth to taste her, lick her, nip her. His chest grazed her breasts, her delicate curves arching hard against him as she pressed deeper into him.

Her response was everything he wanted, everything he could have hoped for, and the damn reception of hers was just a minute farther up the road. But his heart slammed in his chest in a victory dance, his body too caught up in the feel of hers to get the message that this was not the time to take all he wanted.

Damn. Damn.

"Sofia." He kissed her neck below her ear, bit the tender earlobe just above her earring and forced himself to lean back. "We're here."

Eight

Games and lies, Sofia reminded herself later that night while Quinn fielded another question about their relationship from the reporter who wanted to do a follow-up interview with her and her fiancé. They were seated in a private room off the skylight lounge where City Ballet was holding the party for Idris Fortier, the music from a chamber orchestra filtering in through the open door along with the sounds of laughter, clinking glasses and the rumble of conversation.

The space was crowded and warm, especially for those who danced.

Or those who were overwrought with the sensual steam of longing.

Quinn and Sofia had been dealing in games and lies all week, so she could hardly be upset with her handsome, charming date for spinning a moving tale about how he fell in love watching her dance. She'd signed off on the story, after all. She'd agreed that it was easier to root the lies in some element of truth so they had shared memories to trot out at moments like this.

How could she fault Quinn now for being a much better liar than her, especially since she was the one who'd pressed for the pretend engagement?

"But I won't take the focus away from Sofia's dancing," Quinn was saying as they sat side by side on a black leather sofa in the sparse, modern room full of bistro tables and areas for private conversations. "If you'll excuse me, I'll let her finish up the interview." He turned toward her, his tuxedo not showing a single crease as he stood and kissed her hand. "Save me the first dance when you finish?"

His blue eyes had a teasing light. It bothered her that he was good at this, rousing suspicions of his motives no matter that he claimed to be attracted to her.

"Of course. Thank you." She smiled up at him, playing her part but knowing she wasn't as skilled as he was. And her body still hadn't completely recovered from the kisses in the limousine.

If he hadn't pulled away when he had back in the vehicle, she would have sacrificed the most beautiful gown she'd ever worn to press herself against all that raw masculine strength and follow where the attraction led.

"Your future husband was one of the city's most eligible bachelors, Sofia," the reporter—Delaney—

observed. The woman's eyes followed Quinn as he strode out the open door into the party in the lounge. "The McNeill heirs are rich, charming and exceedingly good-looking." She tore her eyes from Quinn as she picked up her digital tablet where she'd been taking notes. "His brother must have made quite an impression on you when he proposed at the airport. But I'm surprised you dated Quinn for so long without meeting Cameron? Cameron tends to be the most visible of the three."

Sofia fought back nerves, not wanting to drop the ball after Quinn had set her up so skillfully to talk about something else.

"That may be, but I don't have much time outside of ballet for socializing. What time I do have, I spend with Quinn. But I'd prefer to talk about work, if you have any questions for me."

Delaney pursed her lips in a frown.

"Very well." She changed screens on the tablet. "Perhaps you'd like to address your critics. Your work has been called mechanical and without artistry. What makes you think you will capture the leading role in the Fortier project when the choreographer is such a decided fan of mood and emotion in his work?"

The biting tone of the query told Sofia just how much she'd accidentally offended the reporter by asking to change the subject. Maybe she should have asked Jasmine to be here for this follow-up interview to help smooth over awkward moments and ensure Sofia didn't embarrass herself. But it cost enough just to have Jasmine set up these kinds of appointments, and she had attended a video interview earlier in the week.

The upside of all the press coverage was that she ought to have a great feature piece by the time they were finished, right?

"I strive every day to balance the physical demands of the dance with all the artistry I can bring to each piece. I hope that I'm always improving on both fronts. An artist should always aspire to improve." She should explain how. Give the reporter more to work with. Except that her nerves had returned in full force.

"And what is your impression of Mr. Fortier so far?" the woman asked, tapping her stylus on the tablet.

Was she waiting for the quotable bit that would torch Sofia's career for daring to stick to the topic?

"I have the same impression everyone else has. He's a brilliant talent and our company is extremely fortunate to work with him." She couldn't believe she'd invited this woman to her private audition with Fortier.

The last thing she needed was to be nervous on that day, too. She was usually so solid when she danced. She didn't need Delaney getting in her head.

"Are you aware that his last two featured leads have moved in with him during the creative process?" The woman watched Sofia's reaction closely. "That he was romantically linked to both of them?"

She hadn't known about that. Although she had read about the affair with the previous one, she'd assumed that was just a one-time thing. People working together fell in love all the time.

But the same scenario twice?

"No." With an effort she coaxed her lips into a smile. "I'm sure it's not a requirement for the job."

Outside the private room, the chamber group paused in their play and someone took the microphone. Sofia peered over her shoulder, wondering if Idris was about to be introduced.

"I'm sure it's not." Delaney gestured toward the open door. "But don't let me keep you. I plan to speak with several more of your colleagues tonight."

"Have you got all the material you need?" Sofia had hoped for a feature in the magazine, not a snippet about her engagement to a hedge fund manager.

"Plenty." Delaney flipped off her tablet and stood. "And I'll be there to film your audition for Mr. Fortier, which will be something our readers will want to hear all about."

Sofia knew she'd made a misstep with the woman, but had no idea how to correct it now. She settled for being polite as she rose to her feet.

"Thank you, I look forward to it," she lied, although not nearly as well as Quinn could have in this situation. Funny how he'd become her biggest ally this week, their unlikely partnership providing her with an outlet at a stressful time in her career.

Maybe she shouldn't be so quick to write off his ability to put on a façade in public. She would do better to learn the trick from him.

"Enjoy that handsome fiancé of yours," the reporter called after her. "You're so lucky to have found someone special. I was thinking of resorting to a matchmaker myself."

Sofia nearly tripped over her feet, the shock of the words like an icy splash to her nerves. Turning, she saw Delaney tapping her chin thoughtfully with her stylus.

"You don't happen to know any good ones, do you?" the woman asked.

A gauntlet had been dropped.

Sofia understood the implication. The woman knew something about what had happened at the airport. Had she learned that Sofia's father had hired a matchmaker? That in itself was certainly not a big deal. But what if she knew more than that? That her engagement was a lie. That Sofia had only done it to quiet the gossip among her peers so she could focus on her dancing.

Maybe she should have straightened it out that night. Stuck with the truth. But since she was in no position to untangle any of it right now, Sofia simply smiled.

"I don't, but I've heard that's a very popular option these days." She rushed to melt into the crowd and find Quinn.

In the pressure cooker of her work world, her fake fiancé had become her best source of commiseration.

And he wanted to be even more than that. He wanted to give her pleasure, a heady offer that had teased the edges of her consciousness all evening long. With her heart ready to pound out of her chest, she realized he was the only person she wanted to see right now.

If only she could truly trust him. But even as she raced to find him, she reminded herself to be careful. He might genuinely be attracted to her. But he wouldn't be helping her right now if it didn't serve McNeill interests.

"I need to speak to you."

Sofia's whisper in Quinn's ear was the sexiest thing he'd heard since that small gasp she'd made in the limo when he'd kissed her neck. He'd been ready to get her alone ever since then.

Maybe this was his moment.

He stood on the fringes of the crowd listening to the guest of honor speak at a podium about his eagerness to work in New York and to let the city inspire him. The guy said all the right things, but something about him irritated Quinn from the moment he'd opened his mouth. Perhaps it was just because he held power over Sofia's career and Quinn didn't like thinking that the subjective opinions of one man could mean so much to her.

More likely, it was because Idris Fortier laughed at his own jokes and occasionally referred to himself in the third person. The well-heeled crowd in attendance hung on his every word, however.

"Should we listen to this first?" Quinn asked Sofia quietly, surprised her interview had finished so soon.

"The reporter asked me if I could recommend a good matchmaker." The soft warmth of her breath teased over his ear, but the seductive sensation couldn't cancel out the anxiety in her words.

And no wonder she was nervous.

"He's almost done speaking." Quinn wrapped an arm around her waist, to bring her as close as possible, wanting to give every appearance of being deeply in love and lost in one another. "It will be easier to talk once the dancing begins." His lips moved against the silk of her hair. "And I don't want your reporter friend to see us darting off in a corner to whisper."

Nodding, she relaxed against him ever so slightly. That small show of trust was something he'd been working hard for all week long. He'd put her needs first, letting Cameron fly to Kiev to handle the hotel acquisitions. He'd asked his brother Ian for help running down more information about Mallory West, giving himself more time to gain Sofia Koslov's trust.

To help her, of course. They'd agreed to as much. But things had gotten more complicated as he admitted the depth of his attraction. He wanted her. And after the heat they'd sparked in the car on the way over here, he thought he knew where things were headed between them.

Would she act on that attraction if she knew this engagement was helping him as much as it helped her? That he'd purposely delayed drawing up that contract he'd discussed with her that first night they'd met because he now wondered if the relationship could help him around his grandfather's marriage dictate.

Quinn still hoped he could help Malcolm McNeill

see that he didn't need to call the shots in his grand-sons' love lives. That he could trust them to find spouses on their own terms and in their own time. Quinn would at least try to talk him into scrapping the marriage stipulation from the will. But failing that? He was confident he could work out some kind of agreement with Sofia that would help him to ful-fill the terms.

As the crowd around him erupted into applause for the choreographer, a violinist struck a dramatic, quavering note. It cracked through the air, stirring the room. The unmistakable trill of a Spanish bando-neon followed in the opening note of a tango, a rare dance Quinn knew well. It transported him back to the small Buenos Aires pub where he'd learned the steps afterhours with his work crew while oversee-ing renovations on one of the family's resorts. He recalled the packed dance floor crowded with pas-sionate couples and knew, with fierce certainty, that he wanted to share this with Sofia.

"Dance with me," he murmured in her ear, his nos-trils flaring at the vanilla scent of her skin. It rose around him and heated his blood.

Her large gray eyes were hesitant, questioning as they swerved to his. He trailed his fingertips up her spine, feeling the sweet curve of her back through silk. "I am classically trained," she murmured in a breathy rush. "The tango is a ballroom dance."

"Then it will be a welcome chance for me to part-ner you on the floor." He drew her toward the square parquet tiles near the musicians.

"Since when do hedge fund managers learn sexy Argentinian dances?" She was light on her feet as she backed into position, joining the handful of couples taking the floor.

"I must have known I'd need to impress a woman one day." He tightened his grip on her, urging her closer as they entered the counterclockwise flow. Her lithe body moved gracefully against his, but this wasn't a pretty dance. It was primal and raw.

She watched the other dancers long enough to gather her bearings, then turned her gaze back to him.

"You are full of surprises, Quinn McNeill." For an aching moment her body cradled the growing hardness concealed by his tuxedo. Then she twisted her hips sideways and kicked her foot through the long slit up one side of her dress, shooting him a coquettish look from beneath the sweep of her long lashes.

At last he'd distracted her completely. She was no longer worried about the reporter, the choreographer or her career. All her focus was on him.

The throbbing notes of the violin wove with the cry of the bandoneon and echoed the seething heat she stirred inside him.

Before she could slip too far away, he hauled her close again then bent her backward. Her spine arched and her head dipped to the floor, exposing the creamy, satin skin of her elegant neck, the slender column of her body. Their hips brushed as they swayed and then he snapped her upright so that their mouths touched. They breathed each other in and their gazes tangled.

Tension whipped between them. His body grew

taut; need and craving pounded through him. He felt the pressure of it all licking through his blood. When he stepped with his left foot, she followed, her limbs seeming to loosen and grow molten, her movements more languid. The arm curled around his neck singed his flesh and her fingers burrowed into his hair, her nails raking his skin.

He steered her expertly, felt her respond to the lightest of touches, the smallest pressure. She seemed to surrender to the dance, to him, as her eyes closed and she let him lead her the way he wanted to.

Yet just when she looked defenseless, a staccato rhythm seemed to break her trance and she whirled around him, improvising mouthwatering steps as he stood rigid, watching. Wanting. He couldn't tear his eyes off her. She held his hand then shimmied lower, her body sinuous. She rose slowly. Out of nowhere, her lips curved into a tempting smile, her expression full of promise.

His mouth dried and his tongue swelled. They cross-stepped for several more beats and the world fell away. His senses narrowed, homing in on the beautiful woman who didn't back down when he pushed forward, who stood her ground and stalked him as well until at last, they stood, foreheads pressed together, breaths coming in fits and starts as the tango ended.

"Come home with me," he commanded. Her eyes burned into his and dimly he heard another song, slower, strike up.

Her grip tightened on his. "Yes."

Victory surged through him. He wanted to pick her up and carry her out of the crowd and downstairs to the waiting limo this minute. But he didn't want to end her time at a work function without accomplishing one more key goal that her friend Jasmine had clearly laid out as an objective for the evening.

"Excellent." He released her slowly, peering through the crowd to find the man who held Sofia's professional future in his hands. "We'll pay our regards to the man of the hour and then we're free to spend the rest of the night however we choose."

He felt her go still beside him. But she didn't tremble or fidget the way she had earlier in the evening.

"Good idea." She nodded. "I'll say hello and then I'll text Jasmine from the car to let her know about Delaney's comment to me. I want to give Jasmine some advance notice if the reporter plans a story about the matchmaking mix-up."

"I'll ask my own public relations department to circulate some stories about our engagement, as well."

That would lend their union all the more credibility. And for the first time Quinn found himself wondering what Sofia would say if he asked her to extend a fake engagement into a year-long marriage like his grandfather's will stipulated…

But of course he wouldn't do that. His grandfather's terms were out of line and unfair. He needed to talk him into rewriting the will. Right now, he would keep his focus on Sofia.

They stood waiting while an older woman dressed in an exotically colored caftan finished her conversation with the famed choreographer. When Sofia turned worried eyes toward him, Quinn took great pleasure in skimming a touch along her hip. And discreetly lower. Her eyes went wide so that she was thoroughly distracted by the time the older woman bid Fortier good-night.

"Sofia Koslov." The boyishly built Frenchman opened his arms wide. "My dear, I've been dying to meet you."

Quinn released her so she could be swept into a hug he personally found too damn enthusiastic, but then, he might have thought as much about anyone who put their hands on a woman he wanted this badly.

"Welcome to New York, Mr. Fortier," she greeted him. Her wooden delivery was an endearing sign of her nerves, Quinn realized.

He liked knowing things about this very private woman that other people didn't.

"Call me Idris. I insist." The man didn't spare a glance for Quinn as his eyes raked over Sofia with what Quinn hoped was professional interest.

Her body was the medium for her dance, he reminded himself even as he ground his teeth together.

"Idris," she corrected herself with quiet seriousness. "We are thrilled to host you at City Ballet. We are all excited to hear your plans for your new work."

Quinn found himself hanging on her words, wanting her to succeed since it clearly meant so much to her.

"And I sincerely hope you will be the first to hear those plans, Sofia. I look forward to your audition."

Before Sofia could reply, the celebrated choreographer turned to greet a young man who'd come to stand behind Sofia, effectively dismissing her.

Sofia tucked against Quinn's side with gratifying ease, whispering, "Did I offend him?"

If she wasn't so intent on securing the man's good opinion, Quinn might have told her that—on the contrary—Fortier's behavior had been rude. But he didn't want her to worry.

"You were perfect," he assured her honestly as he guided her through the crowd toward the coat check. "Jasmine would have been thrilled."

"Speaking of Jasmine." Sofia opened her purse and withdrew her phone. "I need to let her know what happened with that reporter." She lowered her voice for his ears only. "We should be prepared if the woman releases a story about me using a matchmaker."

Quinn nodded his agreement as he excused himself to retrieve their coats. But he already knew his plan B if the matchmaker story leaked. If anyone questioned the legitimacy of their engagement, it would pave the way to convince Sofia to marry him for a year and secure that damned inheritance anyhow.

Just in case.

Nine

Twenty minutes later Sofia watched the numbers light up above the elevator in Quinn's building as they waited for the private conveyance.

Ten, nine, eight...

Quinn's hand brushed the small of her back and circled, his touch burning her as it had on the dance floor. The white-gloved bellhop near the concierge desk spoke with a deliveryman wheeling in a silver cart full of insulated dishes—presumably a five-star meal from an area restaurant. Behind them, an elegantly attired elder gentleman strode through the building's thick glass doors, the smell of diesel and roasting nuts carrying on the rush of crisp, evening air that trailed after him.

Was she out of her mind for being there?

Probably.

Their arrangement was for public events only, yet here she stood, ready—no, *wanting* this intimate privacy with Quinn.

Seven, six, five...

Every nerve ending had come alive since the moment he'd guided her through the most passionate dance she'd ever performed. Only, it hadn't been a performance. Every unchoreographed move had been born out of the sensuous desire he'd incited. Never before had she completely let go that way and she felt so empowered. Impassioned.

Nearby, other elevators with more white-gloved attendants took patrons to their floors, but she and Quinn were waiting for the private one direct to his floor.

Four, three, two...

Yet she hadn't come home with Quinn just because she was crazy with lust. She wanted to take this risk with him and open up as she had on the dance floor. He'd helped her navigate a stressful time in her life just as he'd led her through the tango—with certainty, command, giving as well as taking.

While she'd appreciated his strength and cool head this week, his passionate moves had given her another glimpse at the enigmatic man, made her want to know him more. Following his lead, as she had earlier, gave her confidence to let go and trust that he wouldn't let her down.

In fact, she suspected he would bring her to greater heights than she'd ever known. Her past relationships

had all been as careful as her professional life, each
step rehearsed until she felt safe about moving forward. And where had that gotten her?

It had been bloodless companionship that amounted
to little more than friendships, causing her peers to
think she led some kind of sad, passionless existence.

There was nothing passionless about what she felt
for Quinn. Nothing scripted. Just heat and wild fire.

The elevator bell chimed, the doors opened and
he ushered her inside the wonderfully empty space.
She held her breath as the door swooshed closed and,
in an instant, he backed her up against the paneled
wall. Hand burrowing in her hair, he loosened the
few pins that held its shape so that the fragrant locks
tumbled around her face, releasing the scent of her
shampoo. Her cape slid from her shoulders to pool
on the floor and she shoved his wool overcoat off in
a quick, deft sweep.

She melted at his appreciative, predatory growl.
When his lips brushed hers, she rose on tiptoe and
fit her body against the hard length of him. A feminine thrill shot through her when he deepened the
kiss. His tongue slid over the seam of her mouth,
demanding entrance, and she moaned in the back of
her throat. She felt winded, light-headed and incredibly turned on as he crushed her to him, his mouth
slanting over hers, their tongues tangling in their own
passionate dance.

His heart drummed against her chest, hard enough
that she could feel it through his tuxedo jacket. Her
head tipped back at the crescendo of sensations as

he dropped his mouth to the crook of her neck, his tongue sweeping in intense, hot circles, his breath sounding harsh in the small space.

She gasped when he traced the outline of her rib cage through her dress. Her breasts swelled and ached as his fingers skimmed over her neckline before dipping inside to tease each tight peak. A sizzling tremble ran rampant through her body. His blue eyes burned into hers when the elevator lurched to a halt and he stepped away.

She pressed her hand to her chest as though she could slow the runaway beat of her heart. This was all going so fast, but she needed that speed now that she'd made up her mind not to wait anymore. She'd wanted Quinn, probably had from the moment he'd captivated her full attention at the airport even through her jet-lagged exhaustion. No more holding back. Their tango had been a prelude of what was to come and she wouldn't waste another minute out of his arms now that she'd made the decision to take this risk.

To trust her partner.

When the elevator arrived at his floor, he backed her inside the apartment, guiding her through the vaulted great room and open kitchen that she remembered from the first time she'd been there. Tearing at each other's clothes, they moved as one down a hallway she hadn't seen before, and into a dimly lit bedroom where a lamp shone on a large painting of the Manhattan skyline. In the sitting area, she spied a large desk against one wall and a bank of shade-covered windows on another. When he made as if to tumble them both to the bed, she sidestepped at the last minute.

Just long enough to catch her breath.

Her lips burned from his kisses, her skin tingling everywhere underneath the sensuous silk gown he'd had delivered to her apartment today, complete with a tailor to ensure the hem fell just right. Then the gown had felt like a lover's caress against her skin, the hand-sewn, designer original a decadent luxury. But now, she only wanted the real thing—Quinn's hands all over her. No extravagant dress would do.

"Are we moving too fast?" he asked, brushing his knuckles down her bare arm. "We can slow things down. Take our time. Would you like a drink?"

"No." She didn't need anything to cloud her head. "I just want a moment to take it all in. Savor the sensations."

She rested her hands on his broad chest, admiring the contrast of her pink nails against the crisp white tuxedo shirt, her glittering ring a reminder of all they pretended to be to each other. But she needed this much to be real.

He lifted her hand to kiss the back of her knuckles. The back of her hand. The inside of her wrist. Even that brush of his lips in such an innocuous spot made her simmer inside.

Somewhere in the suite of rooms, a clock chimed twelve. A fairy-tale time…only she wasn't turning into a pumpkin or the girl she'd been before tonight.

Now that she'd stepped onto this path, she was desperate to see where it led. What she would discover.

Most of all, she wanted to dance with him. The kind of dance they'd begun at the party and would continue here to its fiery conclusion.

She turned her back and peered over her shoulder. "I might need a hand." She pulled her hair to one side, revealing the zipper. "I want to be careful with the gown."

"Damn the gown." His teeth flashed in the darkened room. "I want what's inside." He eased the zipper down past her hips and she felt the room's temperate air caress her bare skin.

"Are you sure?" She slid the fabric from one shoulder and smiled at him, loving that he let her go at her own pace, giving her time to enjoy this kind of teasing pleasure.

"Lady, I've never been more sure of anything in my life," he growled, unadulterated male appreciation roughening the edges of his voice. Still, he held himself back and she loved the command he exerted over every aspect of his life—even hers. It steadied the out-of-control tilt of her world and made her feel as though she might stop spinning for tonight at least.

The silk whispered as the gown fell around her silver heels. She stepped out of it then turned slowly. He gaped at her, his amusement gone, replaced by an intent, hungry expression that made her stomach clench and warmth pool at the apex of her thighs. As a dancer, she'd always been aware of her body. She'd felt every muscle, sinew and bone, commanded them to move and pose at her will. Yet now she felt less in control and more aware of her body than ever. Stand-

ing there half-nude in her black lace bra and panties, she felt her skin heat everywhere his gaze fell.
With Quinn, she wasn't just a dancer but a woman
brimming with desire and needs that transcended
her ambitions, her career, her future. She wanted to
gulp down every second of this encounter with him.

When she slid each bra strap down over her arms,
his eyes grew hooded. Exhilaration fired through her
at his reaction. She commanded attention in a way
that had nothing to do with her training, her skills,
and everything to do with who she was…or maybe
who she was discovering herself to be.

She turned again, unhooked her bra then dangled
the scrap of lace from an extended hand, letting the
lingerie drift to the polished wood floor. At his gut-
tural groan she smiled, pressed an arm across her aching breasts and turned, crossing one leg over the other
as his eyes drifted down then rose slowly, lingering.

"Enjoying yourself?" She stepped between his legs
and her knees brushed the edge of the bed.

"Not as much as I'm about to," he vowed then
tumbled her down on top of him.

Sofia absorbed the feel of him, from the hard
planes of his chest through the starched cotton shirt to
the silken glide of his pants along her bare thighs. The
metallic pinch of his belt buckle pressed against her
abdomen, just above the jutting length of his erection.

He cupped her bottom, fitting her to him in a way
that aligned the neediest part of her with that strain-
ing length.

"I've thought about doing this," she admitted,

skimming a finger along the edge of his jaw. "All week, I thought about it when I was on the phone at night with you."

"When we were talking about the missing matchmaker? Our career hopes and the demands of ballet?" He captured her finger in one hand and brought it to his lips for a gentle bite. "All that time, you were thinking about being naked on top of me?"

"Maybe not every second. But the idea definitely crossed my mind a few times. Especially right after I disconnected the calls." Those had been oddly lonesome moments. She'd felt a growing attachment to him but she hadn't been sure if it was friendship, a sense of being allies at a time when they needed one another, or if it was simply attraction. But each night when confronted with the silence of her apartment, she'd thought about how much she wanted to see him again.

Touch him. Undress him.

His expression grew serious. "I thought about you then, too. It was like the quiet echoed louder once we stopped talking."

His words so nearly matched the way she felt she fought a desire to squeeze him tighter and kiss him senseless. She was already taking a risk tonight in being with him. She wasn't ready for a more emotional leap that might bare too much of her soul.

So, instead, she kissed him.

And for the first time she took the lead in the kiss, exploring the fullness of his lips and taking teasing swipes at his tongue. She tasted and tested, liking the feel of his body under her as she moved around him. Her nipples tightened at the friction of the pleats on his shirt. Her hair slid down to pool on top of him, curtaining them in silky privacy. She could have kissed him for hours, but then he ended the game by rolling on top of her.

A new game began, becoming hotter and more fervent until she became lost in him and the way he made her feel. He palmed her breasts, cradling each in turn as though they were precious weights, his thumb gliding over each tip until the peaks ached with sensitivity. Only then did he lower his tongue to first one, then the other, making her back arch to increase the delicious friction.

She lifted her hands to his shirt, flicking open the buttons and tugging the fabric from his pants. He must have loosened his tie and the top button earlier, because the knot slipped free easily, his shirt suddenly open to her questing hands.

He felt even better than she'd imagined, his bare skin simmering with heat. From the sprinkling of hair on his chest, she followed the lightly furred line down the center of his abs to his pants, but he reared up on his knees and stopped her, unfastening the buckle himself and lowering the zipper to her avid gaze.

Built like an athlete, he had the thighs and butt of a soccer player, his whole composition heavier than a dancer's. Sturdier. Immovable. And yet he'd been light on his feet when he'd taken her around the floor in that surprising tango tonight. Proving he knew how to use all that muscle to enticing effect.

"I want you inside me." She didn't know she'd said the words aloud until her throat rasped on a harsh breath. Reaching to touch his hip, she followed the path of his boxers as they slid from his thighs.

"And I can't wait to be there." He stretched over her, his thigh parting hers as he gave her more of his weight.

Sofia sighed into him, wrapping her arms around his neck, molding her breasts to his chest and fitting her hips to his. He rolled them, as one, to the side of the bed where he tugged a box of condoms from a nightstand drawer. He left them there, a tangible assurance she would get what she wanted.

She cried out when he shifted against her, his thigh pressed at the juncture of hers where she ached for him. Where she wanted more of him. But in an instant, he replaced his thigh with his palm, his fingers playing lightly along the damp silk of her panties, now the only scrap of clothing between them.

Their gazes collided in the half light and the intensity of his expression quieted her hunger for a moment since she could see the same need in his eyes. He wanted her, too. Badly. But he must be holding back for the right moment, spinning out the beauty of the dance until act three instead of jumping straight to the climax.

Who would have thought she'd be the one desperate for more, faster, while Quinn took his time with every delicious sensation, burning this night into her memory—she knew—forever. So, closing her eyes, she gave herself over to him and his sure hands, allowing her mind to savor each shock of pleasure he ignited with his fingers. He pressed gently, testing what made her sigh and gasp, only sliding beneath the silk when she twisted her hips in a silent plea.

And, *oh*.

The slick glide of one blunt finger down the center of her set off one heady contraction after another, her body racked with spasms in a release that shook her to her toes. The waves of pleasure broke over her again and again.

Quinn whispered sweet words in her ear, beautiful encouragement she only became dimly aware of as she floated back from her brief trip to carnal oblivion.

"I can't wait to taste you," he breathed against her ear, the sensual promise alone almost sending her body into another orgasmic frenzy.

"I'm too new to this," she reminded him. "That is, I'm not *totally* new to this, but it's never been like this for me before." She kissed his shoulder, her tongue tasting a hint of salt on his skin. "I might lose consciousness if I have much more pleasure in one night."

He grinned, his male pride evident as he tightened his hold on her waist. "I don't think that's possible, but it could be an interesting experiment."

"I think I'd rather be fully in control of my senses for all of this." She roused herself to draw the arch of her foot up the back of his leg, gratified to see his smile slip, his pupils dilate. "You could take it easy on me this first time."

"As long as there are more times." Hooking a finger in her panties, he dragged them down and off, the action stirring a feather that must have fallen in the sheets from her discarded dress.

Quinn plucked it from the air, drawing it over her hip and up her rib cage, circling her breast. Sweet chills skipped along her nerve endings.

"There will be more times," she promised, knowing this night had to mean something more than simple pleasure. Didn't it?

Refusing to overthink it, telling herself that simple pleasure might be a very good thing, she helped herself to the box of condoms and withdrew a single packet.

Handing it to him, he set aside the feather and went to work ripping open the foil. She took the opportunity to kiss along his biceps, feeling the muscles flex against her lips as he moved. The raw power in his body fueled the fire in her.

When he positioned himself between her thighs, she bit her lip at the sensation of him right there, where she needed him most. Their eyes met. Held. He gripped her hips with one hand and tilted her chin toward him with the other.

Brushing her lips with his, he took his time entering her, letting her get used to the feel of him. Even if it hadn't been a long time for her, it still would have felt brand new for being so different. Quinn wasn't like any man she'd ever met and he treated her body in ways no one ever had before.

So by the time they were joined fully, the sweat on his brow told her how much his gentleness cost him. She kissed his cheek and his jaw, grateful for the tender care. But now, with her body easing around him and the delicious pleasure building again, she could give herself over to the sensations. Let him guide her.

Rolling them over again, he settled her on top of him, giving her a sense of control. His hands remained on her hips, though, setting the pace for each toe-curling thrust. For long moments she lost herself in it—the heat of the friction, the musky scent of his skin, the silken sheets that brushed against her calves. But then, remembering the way Quinn's eyes had heated on the dance floor earlier, she swiveled her hips with the grace and strength that a ballerina had at her disposal, taking him with her on a sensual slow ride.

His eyes closed as he hissed a low, ragged breath, giving her a tantalizing peek at the man behind the sleek, controlled exterior. When his eyes opened, she saw blue fire even in the dimly lit room.

Spinning her to her back, he kept one arm anchored beneath her, his forearm aligned with her spine, one hand at her neck. Nose to nose, he thrust deeply—again and again—until the pleasure was too much to bear. She came in a blinding rush, a cry rising from her throat while the spasms trembled through every part of her.

Quinn held her tight, his release following hers a moment later so that his breathing was as sharp and ragged as hers in the quiet afterward. They lay together in the middle of the king-size bed, limbs still twined and sheets wound around their feet in a soft love knot.

Sofia wanted to remain there, boneless and sated, for as long as possible. She felt so good, for one thing. And for another, she had no idea how to follow up something like that with casual conversation. All her life, she'd been better using her body to express herself than her words and she'd done that tonight, as well.

But as Quinn tucked her against his chest and stroked her hair, she knew there was one significant difference.

She'd built some kind of friendship with him, too. That long walk in the park and their talks on the phone at night had all helped her to feel closer to him and to give her the sensation that maybe he cared about more than just protecting his resorts business from the wrath of her father.

She might have been able to drift into sleep on that hopeful note, but one disturbing truth had emerged from the party tonight. As their breathing returned to normal, Sofia couldn't help but share her worry.

"I hope that journalist was just taking shots in the dark tonight when she brought up the matchmaker." She didn't want that story to come out now. Or ever. Antonia Blakely could whisper her gossip all day long, but if there was no proof her father hired a matchmaker, she wouldn't share the story with the media.

Antonia might be venomous, but she wouldn't risk casting a shadow on her own career.

"It seems an awfully specific detail to pick out of

a hat," Quinn observed in a dry voice. He pulled the blankets over her, tucking her in next to him.

Even so, her skin cooled thinking that Delaney from *Dance* magazine might really have her big scoop.

"Jasmine texted me that she'd look into it." Nervous tension crept into Sofia's shoulders, spoiling the languid pleasure she'd been feeling.

"And you know she will. If she has any advance notice, she'll let us know." His hand roved rhythmically along her arm, then rested on her hip. "But if the reporter actually writes that your father hired a matchmaker, we simply toast to the fact that you got lucky on your first try. And then stay engaged for as long as you need to prove you were committed to finding true love." The five-o'clock shadow on his jaw caught against her hair, a tender intimacy that would have soothed her if not for the direction of a conversation that made her worried.

"I can't tie you up forever." She scooted up to a sitting position, her shoulders tensing. "Maybe we should just come clean. It was all a mix-up anyhow."

Quinn shook his head.

"We're in too deep now. And the backlash could hurt my family's business as much as you."

Those tentative, hopeful feelings of trust she'd put in him earlier now seemed misplaced. Quinn really was staying with her to protect his business interests. To ensure her father's goodwill by doing what she'd asked of him.

"So what would you suggest?" she asked, clutching the sheet to her chest.

"If it comes down to it, we can always get married for real." His teeth flashed white in the darkened room, but his expression was more grimace than grin. "No one would dare to question our love then."

"Only our sanity." Frustrated, she debated calling Jasmine anyhow—if only to reassure herself she was worrying needlessly. She wanted real answers, not a glib treatment of the problem. "I'm serious, Quinn."

"Unfortunately, so am I." He leveled a look at her from across the pillow before dropping a kiss on her temple. "Instead of a fake engagement, we make it a fake marriage. We give it a year and call it quits. Our critics are quieted. Scandal averted."

"You would be willing to go that far?" To *actually* marry. "To share a name, a house and a life when it's all for show?"

And she thought she was the performer in the relationship. Perhaps Quinn was a better actor than she knew. Even with her.

"There's too much at stake now. It's not only your career or your father's threats to McNeill Resorts' European acquisitions." His arms went around her, but the temperature in the room had cooled considerably. For her, at least. He didn't seem to realize the effect his words had as he continued. "My name is on a hedge fund. My clients could pull billions of dollars out if they don't trust my word."

She let the realizations roll over her, remembering all the times her mother had warned her to follow her passions and not chase material successes. As much as she'd tried to do that, she still found herself naked in the arms of a man who would always put his fortune first. It was a timely reminder not to wade any deeper into her feelings for Quinn.

But that didn't stop the truth from cutting deep.

Ten

Two days later, Quinn paced around his personal library at the McNeill Fund headquarters in the Financial District, one floor above the McNeill Resorts' offices.

His brother Ian had returned from Singapore earlier in the week. After giving him a day to recover from the trip, Quinn had asked for his help tracking down Mallory West to ask her some follow-up questions after Cameron's too brief interview with her. Ian had texted both Cameron—returned that morning from Kiev—and Quinn to meet this afternoon to share new information that concerned them both.

Now, with Ian leaning a hip on the front of Quinn's massive desk and Cameron commanding the leather executive chair behind it, Quinn stood at the window looking out over the view of the city, the Woolworth Building in the foreground with other towers stretching as far he could see in the wintry, gray haze.

"So is it true that Mallory West closed up shop?" Cameron asked, pushing back from the desk to test the range of positions available on Quinn's leather chair. "When I spoke to her the last time—"

"That wasn't her you talked to." Ian slanted a glance at their younger brother over his shoulder. Closer in height to Quinn than Cameron, Ian had more of their Brazilian mother's coloring—dark eyes and deeper skin tone—but the shape of his face and features echoed the rest of the McNeills.

His clothes were the most casual today—dark jeans with a gray blazer and a button-down. But that was normal since Ian spent most of his time on job sites around the globe.

"Dude. I think I know who I talked to." Cameron smoothed a hand over his bright blue-and-yellow tie that was as unconventional as the wearer. He might sport a Brooks Brothers suit, but his socks were usually straight out of a Crayola box or else covered with weird graphics from video games. "It was the same woman who spoke to me the first time. Who was helping me find a wife."

"Right," Ian told him dryly. "First of all, you don't order a wife the same way you get a snack from the room service menu. Second, the woman you spoke to on both occasions was Mallory's assistant, Kinley."

"She lied to me?" Cameron stopped messing with the settings on the chair and sat straighter.

Quinn pivoted back toward the room, giving Ian his full attention.

"Kinley has been lying to all of Mallory's clients for nearly a year—almost since the inception of Mallory's debut as a matchmaker—impersonating her employer to protect the woman's real identity." Ian hitched his leg higher on the desk so he could face his brothers better. "I'm trying to trace her real identity now. But I wonder if part of the reason the matchmaking service closed down was because something went wrong with Cameron's date."

"But the more relevant question is where did Sofia's contact information originate, and who would have added her to the web site that Cameron viewed?" Quinn asked. "The obvious answer is that it was the matchmaker her father hired, but Vitaly swears the woman he hired speaks little English and was tasked to find a Ukrainian husband for Sofia through personal connections, not online." Quinn wanted to bring reassurance to Sofia after the way things had ended on a strained note two nights ago.

He'd run through the events dozens of times in his mind, trying to pinpoint exactly when her attitude toward him had shifted from red-hot interest back to overly cautious regard. Was it simple morning-after awkwardness? Or had he upset her and not realized it? Whatever it was, he had the sense they'd taken one step forward and two steps back after the Fortier reception.

She certainly hadn't liked the idea of marriage. And he wasn't any more eager to go down that path than her, even if it would fulfill his end of his grandfather's will. But if he had to marry to help Sofia with damage control in the press? Then he'd be an idiot *not* to at least stick with the marriage for a calendar year to take that family pressure off him.

"Are you kidding? If the woman doesn't speak English, it's all the more likely she was confused about what she posted online." Cameron folded his arms on the desk and pulled himself forward on the wheeled chair. "Talk to Koslov's matchmaker and your problem is solved."

"Possibly." Quinn regretted exploring this end of the matchmaking equation more when he'd already guessed it was a dead end. But how much did he dare look into the Ukrainian woman who was Vitaly Koslov's personal friend?

After assuring Sofia he would ask her father to make sure her dating profile was removed from circulation, Quinn had phoned Koslov, but the guy hadn't exactly been forthcoming with much information. All Vitaly had told him was that he'd hired a close personal friend named Olena to search for a husband for Sofia. But when Quinn suggested the woman must have given out Sofia's travel plans to a US matchmaker to relay to Cameron, Vitaly had gotten angry all over again about Cam's public proposal.

"I'm still going to look for Mallory West, just for the principle of the thing." Heading over to the bookshelves, Ian tipped a silver weight that was part of a perpetual motion machine, sending the oddly shaped pendulum piece swinging and glinting in the fluorescent lights.

"Thank you for all you've done." Quinn appreciated the way his brothers came together as a family even if they didn't always see eye to eye. "If Sofia's father doesn't want to come clean about the role he played in all this, I'm not sure I want to ruffle his feathers anyhow. I had one of my IT techs search for any traces of Sofia's dating profile, and he found nothing. So I feel sure her digital privacy is intact."

"It's unlike you to use company resources for something personal," Ian noted while Cameron just grinned. And grinned.

And grinned.

Damn it.

"Obviously the guy needs overtime and I'm paying him out of pocket." Hadn't that been clear? "And what happened in Kiev, Cam? What's the holdup now on those hotels?"

His brother had taken Quinn's place at the most recent round of meetings on the Eastern European acquisitions, but no paperwork had come through for the purchase.

"Officially, we're waiting on some government bureau to sign off. But if you ask me, it's an excuse they trotted out to hide the fact that Koslov is blocking the sale. His name came up more than once during the meeting."

Thwarted on every front, the day was going to hell in a hurry. "Why would he interfere with the deal after I made it clear I acted in his daughter's best interests?"

"Maybe he's waiting to see how it all plays out,"

Ian offered. "She's not off the hook yet, especially if that reporter is hinting that she knows something about a matchmaker."

"Which would be his fault, not ours." Quinn hated having to dance to the guy's tune, but as far as the hotel deal went, clearly Sofia's father had plenty of foreign influence.

Quinn debated speaking to that reporter himself to get a better feel for what was going on. He could run interference for Sofia while she was auditioning since the same reporter would be covering it for her magazine.

Besides, he wanted to see Sofia again. Soon.

His cell phone vibrated on the desk, but before his brothers could use the call as an excuse to leave the meeting, the Caller ID flashed their father's name.

"It's Dad," Quinn announced. "Maybe you'd better stick around."

Both of his brothers went stone silent. Their father communicated with them less than ever since he left the family business. He hadn't been in New York for over a year.

"Hi, Dad," Quinn answered, finger hovering over the button to broadcast the call to the room. "I'm with Ian and Cam. Mind if I put you on speakerphone?"

"No," Liam answered, his voice sounding unusually hoarse. "That will save me having to call them, too."

Concerned, Quinn turned on the feature. "Is everything okay? Where are you?"

A perpetual thrill-seeker, Liam McNeill had gotten himself into some tight spots over the years.

"I'm in China. I figured I'd check out that Mount Hua Shan ascent since your gramps is over here anyhow."

Quinn hadn't heard of it, but he knew the kinds of climbs that attracted his father's attention. "You're with Gramps?"

"Not yet, but I'm heading to Shanghai now. He called me to see if I could come get him out of a local hospital."

All three brothers froze. Quinn could feel the tension in the room as a chill shot over his skin.

"Why?" Ian barked into the phone. "What's wrong?"

"He was on a tour of the city, I guess, and the guide brought him in. There are language barrier issues, of course, but apparently they think he had a minor heart attack and they want to keep an eye on him."

Cameron swore quietly, speaking for every last one of them. No matter his age, Malcolm McNeill had always seemed invincible.

"How far are you from the hospital?" Cameron asked, already loading a map on his phone.

It occurred to Quinn, while his brothers took down the necessary information, that they had taken over his usual role as the leader. He'd froze the first moment he'd heard the word *hospital*.

"Call us when you see him," Quinn barked, finally adding to the conversation. Their father agreed to do so and ended the call.

The three of them didn't say much as they parted.

Their father was already in China, so it wasn't as if they needed to jump on the first plane. He'd let them know if they should come to Shanghai.

After his brothers left, Quinn could think of only one person he wanted to see. Needed to see.

And it wasn't about marriage, damn it, even though honoring his grandfather's will now seemed like something he needed to take more seriously.

Right now, he didn't care about that. He just wanted Sofia's arms around him and he was too numb to think about what that might mean.

The night before the most important audition of Sofia's life, the downstairs intercom buzzed.

"Hello?" she asked, not expecting anyone and figuring it was probably a fast-food delivery guy having a hard time getting in the building. How many times had her neighbor ordered a pizza and then decided to walk her dog or get in the shower?

"Sofia, it's Quinn. I need to see you." His tone set off an answering response in her body before her brain had the chance to think it through.

But something in his voice alerted her that it was serious. This was not the sound of her tango-dancing lover or even her friend who could talk her through her nervousness. Something was wrong.

"Of course." She buzzed him inside and shut down the video of one of Fortier's first ballets she'd been watching. She was dancing a piece from it for her audition, hoping to capture the mood of it better than his star had at the time.

But now her focus shifted to Quinn, as it had so often since they'd met, and even more often since they'd shared a night together. Yes, she needed to guard her emotions more around him. Yet she couldn't simply turn her back on their pact when it had been her idea to stay together for appearance's sake.

Or maybe she just really wanted to see him tonight. The idea seemed like a worrisome possibility as she checked her reflection in a mirror over the couch. Her eyes were bright and her color high. She tugged her black cashmere cardigan closer around her, covering the pink tank top she was wearing with silky, gray lounge pants.

"Get a grip," she reminded herself as she moved toward her front door. She was almost there when a sharp rap sounded.

As she swung the door wide, Quinn's gaze snapped up to meet hers. Everything about him looked tense. His flexing jaw. The flat line of his mouth. The set of his shoulders beneath a black wool coat tailored to his broad form.

And yet some of the tension seemed to ease as he looked at her.

"Sofia." He didn't step inside even though she'd made a pathway clear. "May I come in?"

She waved him in and shut the door behind him. He brought a hint of the cold air with him and a slight hint of the aftershave that she remembered on her skin following the night they'd spent together. Like an aphrodisiac, it pulled her closer and she breathed deep for a moment while she stood behind him.

"Can I take your coat?" Idly, she wondered what he thought of her tiny apartment as she hung the beautifully made wool garment on a simple iron coatrack she'd bought at a salvage shop in Long Island.

She might have connections to Quinn McNeill's extravagant world through her father, but she'd never let herself be a part of it. Last week's ill-fated private flight aside, she paid her own way in life in spite of her father's wealth.

"I apologize for stopping by unannounced. My grandfather had a heart attack twelve hours ago." Quinn's stark statement changed the track of Sofia's thoughts instantly.

"I'm so sorry." She'd never forget the pain of her mother's battle with cancer. The hurts were etched on her forever, pain that went so much deeper than anything her profession could ever wreak on her knees or her feet. "Is he okay?"

She reached for him, needing to offer some kind of comfort in spite of all her warnings to maintain her guard around him. She could never deny someone comfort in the face of that kind of hurt.

"I'm waiting for my father to call from Shanghai with an update, but with the time difference…" He shrugged, still wearing the jacket of his black, custom-tailored suit that looked like something off Savile Row. His burgundy tie and crisp, white shirt were an elegantly simple combination. "I don't know how long it might be." He glanced around the apartment beyond the small foyer. "Am I interrupting anything? I told the driver to wait in case you were busy."

Of course he did. Because hedge fund managers didn't just drive themselves around the city. But even that reminder of their very different lives didn't stop her from wanting him to stay.

"I was just going over some notes for my audition tomorrow—"

"I forgot." Shaking his head, he halted his steps before the living area. "Hell, Sofia. I know how important that is—"

"It's fine. I was only getting more nervous anyhow." She drew him forward, gesturing toward her well-worn couch. "I don't want you to wait for that phone call alone."

No matter that she'd hoped to put up more barriers with him.

He'd been kind to her when she'd been nervous at the reception for Idris. Helped her maintain a façade of an engagement when she'd asked him to. She wouldn't betray their unlikely friendship even if he was better at guarding his heart than she was.

"If you're sure." He still didn't take a seat, however. "I'll stay a little longer." He stopped at a framed photo above an antique wooden rocker. "Is this your mother?"

"Yes." She remembered that moment so well, standing on a rocking boat deck, her mother's arm slung around her shoulders and a new sunburn already making her skin itch. "That's the summer before she died. We went to Greece and sailed with a group of art students around the islands."

"What a year that must have been." He reached to

trace Sofia's face in the photo, a gesture she swore she felt on her own skin. "From so much happiness to mourning her."

"She gave very explicit instructions about that." Her throat tightened as she remembered. "We were supposed to celebrate her life. Not mourn. She wanted her ashes taken out to the Aegean so she could sparkle in the sunlight one more time." Sofia smiled at the memory of her saying the words. "She said if I did it, maybe she'd come back as a mermaid. Which, in all my thirteen-year-old wisdom, I called bullshit. But she said I would understand the truth about beauty and magic when I was older."

"And you have." Quinn turned away from the photo, his eyes full of warmth.

"Not really." She rubbed her arms briskly to ward off a sudden chill despite the cashmere cardigan. "I work hard to create beauty on stage, but I still haven't found anything magical about the sweat, blood and stress fractures that go into ballet."

She hated to sound like a cynic. But perhaps she resented—just a little—that she hadn't inherited more of her mother's free-spirited joy.

"But you saw it that first time you watched *Sleeping Beauty* when you were a girl," he reminded her. "It showed when you told me about that performance. And you admitted yourself that the skill wasn't necessarily impressive. Maybe you only see the magic from the audience."

"Maybe." She conceded the point mostly because she didn't want to bring him down on a night that was already stressful for him. "What about you?" She tugged him to sit beside her on the couch. "Do you see your mom often? I think I read that she's a Brazilian native."

A surprise smile appeared on his handsome face. "Studying up on your fiancé?"

"I had to be prepared to field questions about you since we've been dating for months." She had a lot of her own questions about him. She felt like the man she knew wasn't necessarily the one she read about online.

Lowering himself to the couch cushion beside her, Quinn gave a tight nod. "My mother moved back to Brazil after the divorce. She has a place just outside Rio de Janeiro. I make an effort to call her often, but…"

"But it's complicated?" she offered, touching his hand softly, then linking their fingers.

His mouth cocked into a jaded smile and he rubbed his thumb along the inside of her wrist. "Families are usually more complicated than they seem, aren't they? My parents were married for seven years. My father, for lack of a better description, marches to his own drummer. He's a thrill-seeker, an adrenaline junkie who swept my mother off her feet. He showed up at a bar where she was singing one night after he'd had a close call with a hang glider on a mountain near Rio."

Giving his hand an encouraging squeeze, she nodded at him. "Your mother sings?"

"Not often anymore, but yes. She has a beautiful

voice. The night they met, she thought my dad finally saw the error of his ways and was going to stop taking stupid risks." Quinn barked out a low laugh. "But that didn't last long. By the time the rib fractures healed, he was right back to his old tricks. After seven years together, she said she wouldn't follow him anymore and be complicit in watching him kill himself."

From her quick internet searches, Sofia had read that Liam McNeill was a reckless adventurer. And from what she could tell about Quinn, he was almost the exact opposite. Quinn's practical, steady and calculating nature was probably part of what made him such a successful hedge fund manager. His fund set records two years straight for its profit margins. In some ways he reminded her of her own father.

"Your dad didn't try to change?"

"No. He got a lawyer to divide things up evenly— much to my grandfather's frustration—and my mother returned to Brazil permanently. My brothers and I split our time between Rio and New York. Six months with Dad, six months with Mom."

Sofia's brow rose in surprise. "Do you speak Portuguese?"

"Not as well as I did as a child, but yes. Some Spanish, too. The languages definitely help both my businesses, but I'm not sure I'd recommend raising children on two continents to make it happen." The genuine regret in his voice gave her a small peek into his upbringing and the things he must have overcome. How hard would it have been to be away from his mother for half the year at such a young age?

She wanted to know more about him. But with him sitting so close and her feelings about him all over the map, she didn't know how wise it would be to keep up this intimate conversation when their thighs were almost touching.

Plus, he might ask more about her and her own complicated relationship with her wealthy father.

"A man of many talents," she said, pushing off the couch. "Tea?"

She needed to put some distance between them, even just for a moment, to resurrect some fragile emotional boundaries.

"Please. Thank you, Sofia."

Her apartment was small and she moved quickly from the couch to the kitchen area. Sofia kept her teakettle on her stove for easy access. Filling the yellow kettle with water, she placed it on the burner, twisting the knob to high.

"So that tango at the gala…your globe-trotting background explains why you moved so beautifully. It's part of your identity." Leaning up against the stove, she stared at him, remembering the way his body had kept rhythm with hers.

Apparently going to the kitchen wasn't going to prevent her from wanting him. He looked far too good in her home.

"Yes. But I always gravitated more toward life with my grandfather, who ended up caring for my brothers and me more than my dad. Gramps was the one that pushed me—and my brothers—toward responsibility and productivity. In some ways, I'm much closer to him than I am to either of my parents." His expression darkened. No doubt he was worried about the older man.

"I'm sure we'll hear some news about him soon." She remembered the fear of wondering if a loved one was going to be okay. There were nearly two months of her life she'd spent waiting and terrified when her mother was sick. For the first time she really thought about the fact that her father hadn't been much comfort. But then, he was one to lose himself in work—the same way he pushed her to do now and then. Work more. Dance more. Move forward with life and quit worrying about what might be, until sometimes she felt like she was pirouetting so quickly her world was a blur—

The kettle whistled, startling her from her thoughts, and she poured the boiling water into two teacups. They, like the kettle, were flea market finds. Mismatched. But sturdy, full of character. Artistry of a different kind. She plopped the tea diffuser into the cups, the jasmine green tea mixture instantly turning the water a pale, spring green.

As she placed the cups on the fancy serving tray—another mismatched item—she felt his eyes on her. Glancing around her apartment, her cheeks flushed.

What did he think of her and her piecemeal apartment when his life operated at a whole different frequency? She shouldn't care. And it didn't matter. But she felt a rush of stiff-necked pride anyhow.

She carried the tea to the sofa, nearly spilling the whole thing when his cell phone rang. The chime seemed to blare through the small space, unnaturally loud. Rushing to settle the tray, she sat beside him as he answered the call.

"Dad." Quinn sat forward on the couch, his elbows on his knees, all his attention focused on the call.

Sofia wondered if she should give him privacy. But what if he needed her? She moved closer to him in spite of everything. Damn it, she would have wanted someone sitting by her any of those times she'd gotten bad reports about her mom from doctors who didn't know who else to tell. Her father hadn't been there, unaware of her sickness since Sofia's mother hadn't wanted to tell anyone.

"So that's encouraging news, right?" Quinn glanced over his shoulder and their gazes collided.

She hoped, for his sake, that his grandfather would make a strong recovery. Quinn listened to his father while Sofia stared at Quinn's broad back. Even now, she wanted the right to touch him, to be the woman who sat by his side and could loop her arm through his whenever she chose. What madness was this that gave her such strong feelings for him so fast?

Her heart thumped hard as she took a careful sip of the scalding tea and tried not to eavesdrop. But she was so very worried for him.

"You sure you don't want me to call them?" Quinn was asking. "Thanks, Dad."

He disconnected the call and set aside the phone, pivoting to look at her.

"It was minor and they are keeping him for two days for observation. Gramps' doctor in New York is being consulted, because even though it was minor, they want to put a pacemaker in."

"Can it wait until he comes home?" Arranging for medical care in foreign countries was a challenge. She and her fellow dancers had experienced that more than once in their travels.

"We'll let his doctor make the call after he reviews the tests from the hospital in Shanghai. But Dad says Gramps looks good." Quinn looked better, too. Some of the tension seemed to have rolled off his shoulders since he'd walked through her door.

"I'm so glad to hear it." She set her cup aside and reached for him. She planned to rub his shoulder, maybe. Or squeeze his forearm.

But as she moved toward him, he opened his arms wide and hugged her. Hard.

"Thank you, Sofia." He stroked her back with his big hands, tucking her against his chest. "I was so damn worried."

She would have replied, but her cheek rested against his chest, preventing her from speaking. His arms still squeezed her tight. She settled for planting a kiss on his shirt to one side of his tie. His body was warm beneath the fabric. She could feel his heartbeat beneath her ear. Hear how it picked up rhythm. For a moment time stood still as she thought about what that rapid heartbeat meant. And how the rest of this night might unfold.

He would leave if she asked him to.

She knew without question that how things proceeded from here was her call. But as she edged back to look up at him, she knew she didn't stand a chance of sending him away. Not when her own heart beat faster and her whole focus had narrowed to him.

He was the only man she'd ever met who could make the rest of her world disappear. And the night before the most important audition of her life, maybe she needed the chance to lose herself in the raw passion only Quinn could give her.

Eleven

He wanted to lose himself in her.

Quinn had tried giving her an out, offering to leave so she could focus on her audition. But she had insisted he stay. And after the hellish worry of the last few hours, he was only too glad to shift gears. All that pent-up, tense energy found an enticing outlet in the irresistible woman beside him.

"Sofia." He threaded his fingers through her hair and pulled her to him.

Everything about her was soft and welcoming, from the cashmere sweater to the creamy-smooth skin beneath. He brushed the backs of his knuckles under the cardigan to trace the edge of her tank top. The slow hiss of her breath between her teeth stirred him, calling him to touch her just the way she wanted. Just the way she needed.

"I've missed you." He'd thought about her so often since their last night together. Had it only been two nights ago?

It seemed like two months. He'd wanted her in his bed every moment since.

"I thought I dreamed how good this felt." She kissed the words into his cheek as she undid the buttons beneath his tie.

Quinn tugged at the knot, wanting all the barriers between them gone. He'd taken off his jacket earlier. Now he cursed French cuffs to the skies and back as he undid one and Sofia unfastened the other.

"It was no dream." He tore the shirt off, tossing it on a slipper chair nearby. "I was there, remember? It was better than anything I could have imagined."

"For me, too." She studied his exposed chest. Her gaze hot and admiring, but he wanted her hands all over.

Closing the distance between them, he lifted her against him, startling a squeak of surprise from her while she wrapped her arms around his neck and— much to his pleasure—her legs around his waist.

"Bedroom." He gripped her splayed thighs, cradling them at hip level as he started walking toward a hallway in the back. Her vanilla and floral scent teased his nostrils, bringing back heady memories of things they'd done that night after the welcome reception.

He hadn't wanted to shower the next day, but wanted to savor her fragrance on his skin.

"On the right," she murmured between kisses, her teeth raking gently down his neck. "Hurry."

Her hands smoothed over his back and shoulders, feeling everywhere she could reach. As she moved, her hair stroked his chest, a tantalizing brush of silk each time. She reached to flick a light switch dimmer as they entered the hallway, casting a warm glow where he'd bared one shoulder.

Black cashmere falling away, he nudged aside the tank top strap with his teeth.

"You taste so good." Selfishly, he wanted to keep her up all night, tasting her and tempting her, driving her to that precipice again and again.

But he knew she needed her rest for the audition. This time together had to be enough for tonight.

"You can tell from just one bite?" she teased in a whisper, the hint of her passionate nature setting him on fire.

"I'm hoping like hell I can confirm the facts." He turned them sideways to edge through a partially open door and into her bedroom.

A very white bedroom. A single bedside reading lamp illuminated a high, four-poster painted white with hints of gray details around the carved woodwork and an eggshell-colored duvet atop floor-length pale linens. An antique chandelier hung over the bed. Even in the dim light from the bedside, the glass prisms cast small rainbows around the room. Behind the bed, there was a triangular bookcase instead of a headboard, hundreds of leather-bound volumes adding the room's only color.

Quinn set her in the center of the bed, hating to let go of her, but giving himself a moment to unfasten his belt and step out of his shoes. Sofia watched him, rolling one shoulder and then the other out of her sweater until she was down to her pink tank top and pajama pants. When her eyes lowered to where he unzipped his pants, his blood rushed south, turning him to steel.

It made the unzipping an effort, but seemed to inspire Sofia to sidle out of the cotton spandex, revealing that she was wearing absolutely nothing underneath her shirt. At the sight of her pink-tipped breasts, he forgot about his pants and dived onto the bed with her, drawing her down into the thick duvet with him.

Her moment of laughter turned to a gasp of pleasure as he fastened his mouth around one taut peak, drawing her in for a thorough exploration. She twisted beneath him, her hips seeking his. No woman had ever lit him up as fast as she did, heat blistering across his back, and they weren't even naked yet.

Hands raking off the rest of her clothes—the lounge pants and bikini panties—he traced the muscles of her bare calves and thighs, hugging her legs to his chest as he worked his way back up her body. He kissed a path along her hips, relishing the growing warmth in her skin and liking that he'd put it there.

Heart hammering, he ignored his own needs to focus on hers. Parting her thighs to make room for himself there, he kissed her deeply. Thoroughly. Listened to every sigh and hitch in her breath to learn what she liked best as he stroked her over and over with his tongue.

He brought her close to release twice, feeling her body go taut and still. Both times he backed off, not ready to finish. If this was his only time to be with her tonight, he wanted her fully sated. Boneless with the pleasure he gave her. But the third time she tensed, her fingers gripping his shoulders, he took her the rest of the way, helping her savor every last sweet thrill until she collapsed beneath him.

Elbowing his way higher on the bed, he undressed the rest of the way while she caught her breath. He retrieved a condom from his wallet before he tossed aside his pants, placing it on the bed nearby. When he was done, he moved to cradle her against him so he could stroke her hair while she recovered. He wasn't expecting her to rise up from the bed like some kind of pagan goddess and straddle him, but she did just that, arching her eyebrows at him as though she was daring him to object.

As if he ever would.

"You're beautiful," he told her simply, watching her as she positioned herself above him.

She bent low to kiss him and retrieved the condom. She unwrapped it and rolled it into place, her touch tempting him far too much. He took deep breaths. Steadied himself.

Damn, but he wanted her. Now.

When she lowered herself on him, he ground his

teeth together to hang on to the moment. And when she started to move, her beautiful body a tantalizing gift, he knew that moment would be seared on the backs of his eyelids forever. She gave him this and so much more tonight.

His body roaring with a new fire, he had no choice but to roll her to her back and hold her there for a long moment. Pulling himself together, he steeled his body for the incredible sensual onslaught of this woman.

After a long pause he kissed her, thrusting deep inside her. She surrounded him with her softness and her scent, her arms winding around his neck, her feminine muscles clamping him tight. Sweet sighs turned to needy cries as he increased the pace, but she met every thrust, driving him higher.

By the time the heat in his blood reached a fever pitch, he'd brought Sofia to that heady precipice again, her body tensing under his. Sweat beading on his brow, he drove inside her once more, propelling them both over the edge.

Breath, limbs and shouts tangling, they held on tight to one another while the pleasure swelled and spent itself. They lay there, heartbeats syncing as they slowed.

Quinn pulled a corner of the duvet over her, covering her pale limbs with the white, downy spread. Her blond hair danced along her jaw as the air shifted around her from the movement of the blanket.

She lay her cheek on his chest and he had a sudden pang at the realization that it all felt too damn right. After the way she'd welcomed him, her care for him extending to his family when she'd urged him to stay until his father called, Quinn couldn't pretend this arrangement of theirs was strictly for show. Something had shifted between them and it was a whole lot more than sex.

He didn't know what it was. But he'd dated women for months without feeling the kind of connection he had to Sofia after a week together. And with his grandfather's health on the line now—because, damn it, the heart attack had scared the hell out of him— Quinn couldn't ignore the idea that had been rolling around his head to cement their relationship.

Too bad she'd already told him that marrying for show was a bad idea. He still didn't understand how that was so much worse than a fake engagement, but he knew where she stood in regard to a fake marriage.

But what if it was for his grandfather's sake?

"I can almost hear you thinking," she said, peering up at him from her spot on his chest, her hair a tousled, sexy mess. "Everything okay?"

Quinn could fulfill the terms of the will and keep her by his side in one move. And maybe help her focus on her career instead of all the drama surrounding her demanding job. It would be good for both of them.

"I have an idea." Shifting her in his arms, he raised them to a sitting position, lifting a pillow behind her back. "And I want you to hear me out."

"I'm ready." She practically glowed from their lovemaking, so it was probably as good a time as any to pitch his idea.

"That night Cameron proposed to you, we were so focused on damage control that we never really talked about why he was in such a hurry to find a wife."

"I thought he was an impulsive guy." Frowning, she raised one bare shoulder in a delicate shrug.

"That's part of it. But he was also unhappy with our grandfather for writing up new terms in his will that dictate each of his three grandsons marry in order to secure a third share of McNeill Resorts. He thought it would ensure the company's future." Quinn felt bad he hadn't told her about it before. But there'd been a lot to learn about each other in a short space of time. He'd been busy trying to acquaint himself with her world while she'd been preparing for her audition and managing the fallout of Cameron's public proposal with the media.

"That sounds…heavy-handed." Sofia straightened beside him, her slight withdrawal feeling like an absence. "Why would he think that forcing his heirs into marriages would give his business more stability? Surely he must know those unions won't necessarily be durable."

"He refused to elaborate on his motives before he left for a month-long trip overseas. Privately, I've wondered about his state of mind, and whether my father's very expensive divorce from my mother was a factor in Gramps' decision." The legal termination of their marriage had made her a rich woman able to live anywhere in the world she wanted. Unfortunately it wasn't anywhere near her sons. "But Gramps had his lawyer unveil the new will three weeks ago and so far he's refused to change it. As it stands, each of our portions of the company will be sold at auction if we don't follow the rules and stay married for at least a year."

The air between them stilled. He felt her body tense further, like a wound spring.

"So Cameron wanted to marry me to save his shares in the company?" Her voice hardened, her eyes wide as she swung on him. "He really was looking for a modern-day mail-order bride. And you knew this all the time? Oh. My. God."

Quinn hadn't expected such a strong reaction, especially since she'd met Cameron in person. His brother—while headstrong—wasn't a bad guy.

"Cameron was the most incensed about the terms because he is close to my grandfather and is most invested in the family business. I think he hoped a rash engagement might make Gramps see he'd pushed us too far." At least, that was the reasoning as Quinn understood it. With Cameron, who knew?

Cameron had yet to give him an explanation that made any sense in his mind.

"So, basically, to hell with me and my feelings. I was just supposed to be the wife of convenience for him." Sofia shook her head, then took a deep breath as if trying to hang on to her patience. "I hope he's not going to try that again with someone else."

The silences between her words seemed to grow longer, more deliberate and awkward. Was he being shut out?

She paused, her voice getting quieter. "What about

you, Quinn? Are you going to marry and follow your grandfather's rules?"

He couldn't read her right now. Didn't know if she was already thinking he was ten kinds of ass for considering it. Or if she could possibly have the same idea in mind as him: that a marriage between them could be beneficial all the way around since she'd been pressured by her father to settle down, as well.

"I wasn't planning on it." He chose his words carefully, well aware he was walking on thin ice here, not wanting to lose what they'd just shared. He still wanted to explore where it might lead. Might? Where it damn well was heading at the speed of light. "But I'll admit that having my grandfather's health in question now makes me rethink how much I want to dig my heels in about protesting the will."

"Meaning?" She lifted an eyebrow in silent question.

"Meaning…" He was in too deep to turn around, but he realized midstream he probably should have prepared more. Had a real ring that was from him and not Cameron. Thought about what to say. But, too late now. He'd come this far already and he was a man used to making executive decisions quickly, firmly, decisively. "Why don't you and I get married?"

How could a man she'd only just met break her heart in such a short space of time?

She'd known Quinn for a week, but it had been an intense time with a lot of personal upheaval for her. Maybe that's how she'd come to care about him far too much, far too quickly. The turmoil had forged a bond between them, yoked them together. The heat of their passion and the high stakes of preserving her public relations campaign had driven her into the arms of a man that could not emotionally provide for her.

He'd slipped around tattered defenses when she was battling injuries, professional jealousy and worries her career could end before she had a plan B in place. Before she knew it, she was opening her heart to a man wholly inappropriate for her.

It wasn't his fault that her heart ached so fiercely she wanted to hold on to her chest to try to ease the pain. No. The fault was all hers for not protecting herself better, especially when she'd known that he was getting under her skin and making her care.

"Sofia?" Quinn's fingers brushed along her jaw, tipping her face up so he could see her better. She wanted to fold into his touch, melt into him again. But things between them had changed. Everything had. "It could solve a lot of problems for both of us. Quiet the speculation about our engagement with the reporters and with your peers so you can focus on the art that's most important to you. And, of course, it would secure my grandfather's legacy and fulfil his lifelong dream for his grandsons to run the company. At least where I'm concerned."

"If he'd really wanted that," Sofia interjected, leaning away from Quinn's touch, the chill of the apartment flooding the space where his fingers had lingered, "he could have just given you each a third of the business."

"I think he wanted to—"

"No," she said, forcing strength into her voice. She couldn't pretend to listen seriously to this idea when Quinn had crushed a piece of her by even suggesting it. "I know I agreed to hear you out, but I understand what you are proposing."

The thought ripped through her, wounding her more deeply than any injury dance could ever give her. Ballet could never betray her like this.

"It would only be for one year," he clarified. "Like dating with incredible benefits for both of us. I could help you solidify your career plans during that time so when you're ready to quit dancing you have a future you're excited about."

He understood her practical needs so well. Unfortunately he didn't have any idea about the emotional end of the equation.

"Most people don't put a time limit on a marriage, but thank you for making that perfectly clear." She shot out of bed, dragging a sheet with her, unable to sit quietly by while he spouted more ideas that were like small knives to the naïve vision she'd had of continuing a relationship. "I really thought we had a connection, Quinn."

Stepping behind a screen, she flipped the sheet over the top because damned if she was baring any more of herself to him. She found her tank top on the floor and yanked it back on. Then she slid her pants into place, desperate to put boundaries between them, any sort of boundary at this point.

"We do. I never would have suggested this otherwise." She heard the creak of the mattress and the whisper of his clothes as he slowly got dressed. "I don't understand why you're so upset."

"I'm upset you never mentioned this will and the need for all the McNeill men to marry, when it feels highly relevant to our arrangement." Stomping out in her tank and pants, she found her sweater and punched one arm through each sleeve. "You even suggested marrying if worse came to worst and the *Dance* magazine writer published something unsavory about me. That would have been the perfect time to clue me in about the will and how—by the way—it would check off some boxes for your goals, too."

"How is me using a marriage to satisfy the terms of my grandfather's will any different than you using an engagement to smooth over your public relations agenda before a big audition?" Quinn stood, his clothes on but his shirt unbuttoned, the tie loose around his neck.

"I was trying to maintain focus on my career during a drama that had *nothing* to do with me. You're trying to protect your bottom line." She lobbed the accusation at him and hoped it found its mark.

"No." A new stillness went over him, alerting her that she'd at last gotten through to him. "Actually, it's about protecting family, which is the most important thing to me."

Watching the pain flash across his face sent a tiny

prick of regret stabbing through her. She couldn't forget how devastated he'd looked when he'd walked into her apartment tonight. But, damn it, he had hidden the truth from her.

"You told me that billions of dollars of investments would be at risk if people don't trust you, but how are you worthy of trust if you treat a person as deceptively as you've treated me?" she reminded him. Reminded herself. She kept having to do that. "So, to a certain extent, it is about the money."

"If it was just about the money, I would find another way. I know it doesn't mean much to you, but I'm fairly good at making it." His mouth twisted. His jaw flexed. "I only care about making sure my grandfather's life's work is not lost to strangers because of his desire to see the family settled."

He waited for her to say something. But she was at a loss, empty after a night where passions had run high. Her emotions were spent and she didn't know what—or whom—to trust.

She stared at the rainbow colors leaping from her engagement ring in the muted light of her bedroom. It was the physical manifestation of every lie and deception.

With more bravado then she felt, she twisted the ring from her finger, hoping that with its absence, she'd be able to focus on why she was here in New York. On why she didn't get involved.

"I'm sorry, Quinn. But I don't know how to move forward from this. I know I asked you to pretend we were engaged to help me, but I release you from our agreement." Handing back the ring, she was done with false promises and a relationship that was just for show.

She'd finally learned to put some trust in her partner, and it had been a mistake that had cost her dearly.

Quinn stared at the ring in his open palm for a long moment.

The moment echoed between them. Her heart hammered; she was wretched. If he would just walk away now, she'd be able to curse him, move on. But he just stood there, a lingering shadow of what could have been.

"I know that people are important, Sofia, not the bottom line." His hand closed into a fist around the ring, the whites of his knuckles showing. "Has it occurred to you that you're so busy seeing the bottom line—in my case, a wealthy one—and that you're not seeing the person behind it?"

His eyes held hers. Challenging her.

"I don't know what I see anymore," she said tightly, barely hanging on to the swell of raw emotions seething just below the surface. She wrapped her cashmere sweater around her like shrink wrap to hold herself together. "I don't know what to believe."

"I'm not going to be the one to break our engagement." He set the ring on a whitewashed narrow console table by the bedroom door. "Keep this in case you need it to stem unwanted questions from reporters about its absence. And good luck tomorrow."

He walked out of her bedroom. Out of her apartment. The door shut quietly behind him. Only then did she allow her knees to give out beneath her. Curling on her bed, she wouldn't let herself her cry. Not when she had the most important audition of her life tomorrow.

There would be time enough for heartbreak afterward.

But as she closed her eyes, a tear leaked free anyhow. Despite her famous iron-clad professional discipline, her body had its limits for what it would do based on sheer will. She could dance on stress fractures and bunions, pick herself up after her dancing partners dropped her on a hard, unforgiving floor that would leave her body bruised for weeks.

Yet she'd discovered tonight that her eyes would go on crying even if she told them not to. And her heart would keep on breaking the longer she thought about Quinn. In spite of all reason and practicality, she'd fallen head over heels in love with this man.

Twelve

Turning around the stage in petit jeté jumps, Sofia prepared to dance for Idris Fortier. The choreographer sat in the middle of the small practice theater, which would be a closed set for the next hour. He'd allowed Delaney to sit off to one side with her camera, but had requested she not film during the session.

Even Delaney had been too cowed by Fortier to gainsay him. Sofia smiled to think how quietly the journalist had slunk to the sidelines to watch Sofia perform.

"Are you ready, darling?" the choreographer called up to her now, his accent lingering over the endearment even though his eyes were still on his tablet screen.

"I'm ready." She'd barely slept the night before

and wondered if her parting with Quinn was going to cost her this audition, too.

The role of a lifetime. The cementing of her place in the ballet world. Some dancers were principals twelve, fifteen or even more years. Sofia knew her knees were on borrowed time. She might come back after the surgeries she would one day need, but a dancer never knew if she would be as skilled afterward.

She needed her career on fast forward in order to have the kind of post-dance life she envisioned for herself. To still work in the field and be able to hold her head high.

"What will you be dancing for me today?" He put his tablet aside and adjusted the small, round spectacles on his nose, giving her his full attention.

Sofia had planned for weeks to dance one of Fortier's dances. A flattering compliment. Plus, dancing a younger choreographer's work meant that there were fewer ballerinas she could be compared to. New pieces allowed a dancer a little more room for interpretation. But after the tears she'd shed last night, she'd arisen from bed this morning with the Black Swan in her heart and ready to burst through her toes.

"Black Swan. The final act in the Grigorovich version." She could dance that one without a partner since there was less emphasis on the pas de deux so important in the Balanchine version.

"An interesting choice, Ms. Koslov. Wholly unexpected."

She had no way of knowing what he'd expected.

But most experienced dancers left the world's most well-danced pieces alone for situations like this since they left too much room for comparison. Today, Sofia did not care. She strode to the side of the stage to start her music, which gave her a twenty-count of silence to walk to position. She wanted to dance the hell out of a virtuoso piece and demonstrate the technical skill her critics all agreed she possessed.

And if she couldn't add the extra layer of emotion that some say was occasionally missing from her work? She didn't deserve the part. Because today, she was nothing but raw emotion with Quinn's parting words still echoing in her head.

You're so busy seeing the bottom line...you're not seeing the person behind it.

As if *she'd* been the one to focus on his wealth.

Banishing the thoughts from her head, she took solace in the music and let Odile's seduction blast away everything else. She didn't want to be hapless Odette who lost Siegfried even though she hadn't done a damn thing wrong. Right now, she needed the fiery passion of Odile to lure Siegfried to his lonely end.

With multiple pirouettes spinning her across the stage, Sofia articulated every phrase, letting the music fill her as she poured out the role. Space-devouring leaps ate up the stage. Fast fouettés flowed naturally, one after the other. She didn't dance so much as she burned—all the heedless energy and longing of the night before torched through this one outlet she understood.

When she reached the end of the coda, the final fouetté perfectly timed, Sofia held her position into the silence, her breathing so heavy the pull of air was the only sound in the theater.

Until one person clapped. The fast, excited clap of genuine praise. And since Sofia could see her evaluator seated, unmoving, before her, she knew it hadn't been him doling out enthusiasm. Had Delaney truly been impressed? It didn't matter, but after tossing and turning about this dance all night, Sofia felt gratified to think someone had liked it. The journalist might be motivated by gossip scoops that would sell more magazines, but the woman would certainly know her ballet.

"Thank you, Ms. Koslov." Idris Fortier rose to his feet and glanced sharply to his right. "I'd like a moment alone with my dancer, please?"

Sofia went to shut off her music while she heard Delaney making moves to leave the theater. As she wiped down her face with a clean towel, Sofia caught her breath and turned to find Idris standing very close.

"Oh." She stepped back to give herself room. "I didn't hear you." Her shoulders tensed; she hated to feel crowded and had anxiety in social situations where the professional pressure was high. For a split second she wished Quinn would show up—

And how ridiculous was that?

Her brief engagement was over, her ring still at home on the console where he'd left it.

"You have my full attention for this position,

Sofia." Fortier's accent—French by way of Tunisia—had a peculiar but pleasant inflection.

"I realize you still have several dancers to audition." She should be pleased, she knew. She'd hoped to impress him and she seemed to have accomplished that.

But why was he standing so close? She folded her arms.

"The part is yours now if you are willing to work hard for it." He took her arms and unfolded them, extending them. He studied her body. "Black Swan really shows off your Russian training. You have beautiful extension."

Her body was part of her art, she reminded herself. Ballet was incredibly physical and she'd been touched often in her career by other dancers, directors and choreographers. So while Idris's touch felt a bit too informal for their first true professional meeting, it certainly wasn't out of bounds.

And…he'd said she had the part? Excitement trembled through her as she became aware of rehearsal music in the next studio over. A group was working on an interpretation of Vivaldi's "Four Seasons."

"I am prepared to devote everything to the project," she told him sincerely. She'd pinned all her professional hopes on it.

His hands lingered on her wrists as his dark eyes met hers.

"What will your new fiancé think of you spending all your time with me?" He didn't move. Didn't release her.

She stepped back, pulling her wrists from his hold but easing any offense with a smile.

"He will be proud of my success." She refrained from mentioning that her engagement had ended. With the strange dynamic at work in the room, she felt that it would be good protection from any misguided notions Idris might have about her becoming his lover, the way his last two featured performers had.

"Will he?" The choreographer narrowed his gaze and backed up a step. "Many new relationships are full of jealousy. That can destroy a dancer's focus."

It would destroy anyone's focus. But she could see his point. Besides, using her relationship with Quinn for show was exactly what she'd said she wouldn't do anymore. She'd wanted honesty about their relationship, not more subterfuge.

"Actually, our engagement is off," she confided. "We aren't announcing it to the press, but it was all so sudden—"

"This is very good news, Sofia." He smiled in a way that unsettled her.

It was almost as if he'd been expecting her to say that. She'd known the man for less than an hour and already she didn't like him. Artists could be strong personalities though. Maybe that accounted for it. And sometimes, the more successful, the more eccentric. Backing up another step, she bent to retrieve her phone, disconnecting it from the external speaker that had played her audition music.

"For me, as well. I couldn't be more pleased to

work with you on a new ballet." When she straightened, he was still there, closer than ever.

His eyes were fastened to her left hand. He picked it up and kissed her ring finger before she could yank her hand back.

"Just happy to see this place is bare and that you are free," he explained, finally stepping away from her. "Let's go to lunch and celebrate the launch of our new partnership."

"I can't today." She hadn't even showered. She'd barely slept. And she had a very strange vibe from him that she needed to seriously consider. "I have another appointment."

"And I thought you were prepared to devote everything to this project?" The man's tone withered.

Damn it. She wasn't going to play this game. She'd worked too hard for her spot at the top of the company to be treated this way—even by a major star of the industry.

"Everything within the bounds of professionalism. And since I knew you had two other dancers to audition, I haven't cleared my schedule yet to begin working on new development."

"Perhaps you shouldn't bother. I can see you're not excited to begin." He gave her body a meaningful look, one she'd seen too often leveled at a dancer desperate for a break.

"If you're looking for a creative partnership, Mr. Fortier, I can't wait to begin." She didn't want to lose the role on a misunderstanding or because she was admittedly testy today.

Then again, she wasn't going to let him touch her, kiss her finger and stare at her body without calling him out.

"What if I'm looking for more, Ms. Koslov? What if I've read your reviews about passionless performances and I think I could be the man to inspire a creative fire that would make you unforgettable in every viewer's eyes?"

Anger simmered. She knew her Black Swan had just contained so much damn passion she'd burned down the room with it.

"How exactly would you accomplish that?" she asked, hearing a scuttling noise in the backstage area.

Had someone else entered the small theater or was that just wishful thinking?

He leaned closer, not touching her, but lowering his voice considerably. "Put yourself in my hands, Sofia, and you will see."

She didn't know if that was intended to be seductive, but she'd had enough of walking the edge of creepiness with him. And maybe her time with Quinn had given her enough confidence in herself to know she had all the passion she needed inside. This man couldn't undermine her with his smarmy insinuations.

A voice niggled at her, making her wonder if she could have walked away so confidently a week ago.

"I wonder if you actively seek out the most insecure women for your games, Mr. Fortier?" She backed away from him. "But I am not one of them, I assure you. I know my own worth. And I can admire your artistic excellence without being madly in love with you. I hope you will respect me enough to do the same for me."

Padding across the floor in her ballet shoes, Sofia left him to splutter condemning warnings about the future of her career. He threatened to tell the world she'd flubbed the audition and that's why she didn't get the part. And while that hurt, she refused to engage with him any further. She gathered her dance bag to change in a more private dressing room when she ran into Delaney.

The reporter held up a quieting finger as if she didn't want to be discovered, then waved her out into the corridor while Fortier ranted about naïve girls who didn't understand the way the world worked. What a disappointment the man had turned out to be. Usually news about people like him—a lecherous creep in the ranks—traveled along the dance grapevine quickly. She wondered if she'd alienated her fellow dancers too much in the past and that's why she hadn't already heard it for herself.

"Sofia, I taped a little of your audition," Delaney confided privately. "And I stayed behind even when he told me to leave—"

"My God." Sofia slammed through another door into a private dressing room empty except for open bags and discarded street clothes; everyone else was rehearsing right now. "Are there any lengths you wouldn't go to in order to get a story?" she fumed.

"No." The reporter set a small disk on the makeup table in front of Sofia. "But in this case, you should be thrilled since this can prove you danced your freaking toes off. You were amazing back there."

"You think so?" So maybe the self-worth she bragged about to Idris Fortier wasn't quite as steadfast as she'd pretended. Who didn't love to hear good reviews?

"I know so. And the footage I got shows it." She tapped the disk. "I heard that bastard threaten to tell people you flubbed it. I couldn't hear everything that happened before that, but it sounded like he was coming on to you?"

"Yes." Sofia dug through her bag for her facecloth. "I tried to tell myself he was just eccentric, but in the end, there was no mistaking he was angling for me to kiss his ass. And more."

"Bastard." Delaney frowned. "I took the footage hoping to use it to persuade you to give me a story about Cameron McNeill using a matchmaker."

"Excuse me?" She set down the cleansing cloth, shaking her head in disbelief.

"I moonlight for a gossip magazine on the side. It pays better." She shrugged, unapologetic. "It's expensive to live anywhere near this city. I was a dancer once, you know. A halfway decent one. But after I got hurt, my options were limited. I'd like to write about ballet and only ballet. But there's no money in it."

"What did you hear about Cameron using a matchmaker?" Sofia asked, needing to know what she was up against. Now that she'd ended her relationship with Quinn, she wouldn't have his help figuring out what to do next.

"Just that he hired Mallory West to find him a bride. I'm going to publish that much, but if you can give me anything else to add..."

"You're trying to trade the audition footage for information?" Sofia was going home and going to bed for a week. She couldn't deal with this toxic environment. Especially not with her heart breaking over Quinn and her career very likely in the dumps now that she'd told off the most respected choreographer of her time.

"I thought about it. But I can't do it." The journalist shoved the disk closer. "I can't stand it when guys try to use their position to manipulate women. Consider this me cheering on your rejection of his slimy suggestions."

"In that case—" Sofia put the disk in her bag along with her pointe shoes "—thank you. I can't help you with any information about the McNeills, though."

"Is your engagement really over with Quinn?" the other woman asked. "Or were you just saying that to convince Fortier you could do the role?" Delaney pointed to Sofia's bare ring finger.

"No comment." Sofia smiled brightly to hide the fact that just hearing Quinn's name hurt today.

He'd been such a generous lover the night before. Could a man so giving in bed really want to deceive her as thoroughly as she'd accused him of doing? She wished she had some perspective on the situation. Later, she would call Jasmine and ask for her best friend's advice. For now, she needed to go home and wrap her sore knees.

"Fine. But if you want my two cents, I would not let that man go." She shoved the strap for her black leather satchel onto her shoulder and checked her phone. "Besides being one of the city's most eligible bachelors, he seems to only date people he really cares about, you know? You won't see his name in the gossip rags, that's for sure." The woman headed for the door, shoving her phone into the back pocket of black jeans under a quilted blue parka. "And there was an older woman looking for you backstage earlier. With an accent. Oleska? Olinka?"

"Olena?" Sofia stilled. Olena Melnyk was one of her father's oldest friends from Ukraine. They'd visited with her briefly in Kiev after one of Sofia's performances. What was she doing in New York?

Delaney snapped her fingers. "That's it. I told her you'd probably be in the main theater after this."

Grabbing her bag, Sofia left the dressing area to peer inside the main theater. She didn't feel guilty about going home for the day. She didn't have any rehearsals scheduled and she'd substituted her audition for a class to keep her limber. The audition had been as physically demanding as two classes— a fierce workout for certain.

"There you are." A voice sounded behind her, the thick Ukrainian accent familiar since it still colored her father's speech.

"Olena." Sofia turned to find the petite, round-cheeked woman pacing the halls outside the theater. "My father didn't mention you were coming to New York. How nice to see you."

Olena wore a red scarf around her head and tied under her chin, the bright silk covering hair that had faded from blond to gray, but still gleamed with good health in the bright overhead lights.

"I go to Des Moines to visit my son. But I stop in New York when I find out your father, he is angry with me." She gestured with her hands, agitated.

Sofia spoke very little Ukrainian, so she was grateful for Olena's English. Although, at the moment, she wondered if her father's childhood friend had chosen the right words. Why would her father be mad at her?

"I can't imagine why he would be." Sofia hadn't spoken to her father since the flight home from Kiev, letting Quinn intervene on her behalf because she'd been so upset with him. She'd been ignoring his calls for days. "He was so glad to see you the night after my performance—"

"He is furious I did not choose Ukrainian husband for you. That I allow New York rich man to meet your plane." Her round cheeks deflated with her frown. "I am so sorry, my girl."

"*You're* the matchmaker he hired?" Sofia leaned into the back of a nearby theater seat, revising her perspective on her father's underhanded scheme.

Something about "hiring" his good friend from the old country—a woman who had helped him with his history homework in grade school—seemed far more forgivable than if he'd contracted an expensive global dating agency. While still underhanded of him, at least there was something personal about the approach.

"Yes." She gave an emphatic nod. "He told me, 'Olena, find our girl a good man.' But afterward, Vitaly very angry I did not choose man from old neighborhood."

"He never told me that he wanted to hire a match-maker." And the more she thought about that, the more she remembered how his pressure to get married had undermined her. As did his insistence she take his money. Had her father been holding her back from becoming self-confident all this time? Yet a voice inside her persisted; something had changed to give her a newfound strength and belief in herself. "And then, my photo and contact information ended up on a web site for men seeking wives—"

"I did this." Olena patted her chest to make it clear. "Come, we walk and talk. I explain where walls do not have ears." She glared at a young ballerina who had come out into the hallway, probably just trying to find a place to smoke.

The girl skittered back into the theater while Sofia tried to process what the woman was saying.

"You posted my photo on a site for men seeking a quick marriage?" Sofia asked as they walked out into the chill of a New York winter, a crust of snow covering most of Lincoln Center.

"My nephew helped. But I am very clear." Olena pounded one fist against the palm of her hand, her heavy silver rings glinting in the sun. "I say, my girl only date men ready to marry."

Sofia closed her eyes briefly, letting that news wash over her. Her father had asked an old friend to find her a Ukrainian husband. Instead, Olena had gone online to advertise her. No wonder Cameron had only gotten half of Sofia's details. The older woman was hardly a professional matchmaker. Just a well-liked woman from her father's hometown.

"So you told someone about my plane landing in New York?" Sofia wasn't ready to fight her way through the crowds on the subway yet. Maybe she'd walk for a while to let the fresh air clear her head and sooth the ache in her heart.

"First, I check the name of the man who asks about my Sofia. Very rich. Very handsome. I give details of flight." She shrugged her shoulders. "But you are not happy?"

Halting on the sprawling mezzanine outside Lincoln Center, Sofia let the snow fall on her as she watched the lunchtime traffic fill the streets. She wasn't about to delve into a long explanation of why she hadn't want her father in charge of her dating life. But she didn't mind sharing why she wasn't happy.

"I am only unhappy that my father thinks he can control my life. That he could manipulate me into marrying a wealthy man who moves in the same kind of circles as him." Her hands fisted inside the bright yellow mittens that a fan had knitted her long ago—a young ballet student who hadn't been invited into the company after graduation. The girl had moved back to Nebraska, but had given the mittens to Sofia as a thank you for inspiring her.

Oddly, looking down at them now made her realize that was a little bit of magic in her career. She'd told Quinn there wasn't any—only hard work. But that wasn't entirely true. Touching someone else's life, making a difference—that was beauty and magic combined. An insight she wondered if she would have realized without Quinn.

"It is not the point to be rich." Olena gripped her shoulders with her weathered hands. "It is the point to be a good man. And this McNeill, he is smart and successful. His smile is kind."

"So the fact that he is wealthy was incidental?" She shouldn't be hung up on it. The fact that she protested it only proved Quinn's point that she was too focused on the bottom line and didn't see him for himself.

Had she made a horrible mistake in sending Quinn away?

"Rich man focus on you instead of struggle to make life for himself. But there are good men everywhere." Olena spread her arms wide to point to the whole city. "You look beyond this small corner where dance is all you do. Find different men who give you new look at world, yes?"

"Yes." Sofia agreed, although in her heart she knew that search wouldn't be happening for a long time.

"Good. Then I have done my job." Olena patted her cheek. "I will not help anymore, as you ask. Tell Vitaly that we spoke, yes? He will forgive me then, I think." The older woman pulled her in for a hug and a kiss on each cheek. Exchanging goodbyes, she turned on her furry boots and stalked toward the subway station through the crusty snow.

Totally spent on every level, Sofia turned toward downtown to start the walk home. She might give in and get the bus in a dozen blocks or so, but right now she needed the fresh air. Striding across the mezzanine, she neared the crosswalk when a black Escalade rolled to a stop at the curb. She wasn't sure why her eye went to it.

But when Quinn McNeill stepped out of the back door of the chauffeured vehicle, she felt his presence like an electric shock.

"Sofia." He beckoned her through a veil of snowflakes. "Can I give you a ride home?"

Her pulse sped, her mouth going dry at the sight of him. How had he gotten more handsome since the night before?

"No. Thank you." She could hardly resist him from ten yards away. She would have no chance of denying him anything if she sat beside him in the warm comfort of that luxury SUV. Especially after Olena's pep talk about finding someone who made her see beyond the confines of her narrow world.

She questioned her feelings for Quinn, what she'd learned from him, but, damn it, this was still so new.

But her refusal didn't make Quinn jump back in his ride and leave. He exchanged a word with the driver before dismissing the vehicle. Then he strode toward her, his long, denim-clad legs covering the space quickly.

Even before he reached her, she knew she was toast. She'd stood up for herself to Idris Fortier. Held her ground with Delaney the nosy reporter. Danced the best piece of her life.

She didn't have the reserves for the temptation that Quinn McNeill presented.

He paused a few inches away from her.

"We need to talk."

Thirteen

Quinn had had his driver circle Lincoln Center for the last hour so he wouldn't miss Sofia after her audition. Jeff had promised to keep an eye on the exits so Quinn could work, but he couldn't have concentrated on anything else anyway.

Thoughts of the woman now standing in front of him had consumed him ever since he'd walked out of her apartment the night before. He'd felt that she'd needed him to leave, so he had. And he'd been offended that she'd reduced their relationship to economic differences that didn't matter. But, apparently, they mattered to her. Today, he realized that if he was serious about her, he needed to take her concerns seriously, too. That meant he was going to do a better job listening and paying attention, not just lining up his questions while already thinking ahead to his next move.

He had a few ideas for how to show her he was committed to her and not some temporary marriage to fulfill the terms of a will. But that's all they were— vague ideas. And he hated not having a solid game plan to win her back. In a short space of time she had become his most important priority and he was shooting from the hip with her.

She defied business logic.

She was art.

She was magic.

And, by God, he wanted her to be his.

"I was going to take a walk," she told him, look- ing so damn beautiful in her dark bomber jacket with a shearling collar pulled up to her heart-shaped face. Her hair looked like it had been in a ballet bun at one point, the ends all wavy and still a little damp. Tall boots covered most of her leggings, so she looked warmer than the last time they'd taken a walk together. Her bright yellow mittens reminded him of the sunny teacups she'd used the night before when she'd made him tea. But she was full of those contrasts—the worldly sophistication next to her more bohemian tendencies made her who she was.

A very special woman able to stand on her own feet.

Or tiptoes.

"I'll go wherever you like," he assured her. "But if we walk through the park again, we might have more privacy."

Also, he hoped traveling that route held happy memories for her, too. He needed every advantage at his disposal to ensure she didn't turn her back on him forever.

"That's fine." She nodded, heading toward Central Park the way they had after the meeting at Joe Coffee the week before.

"How was the audition?" he asked, knowing how much it meant to her. He reached for her bag, but she didn't give it to him to carry and he didn't press her.

"I nailed it," she said flatly, snowflakes swirling around them. "He offered me the role."

"That's incredible, Sofia. Congratulations. But I would have thought you'd be more excited." Maybe she was as tired as him.

Had she spent half the night thinking about the way they'd parted, too? He wished she would have agreed to join him in the Escalade where he could have spent his time watching her expression and gauging what she was feeling instead of looking out for traffic.

"It was clear to me that he expects to have an intimate relationship with his feature lead." She shoved her yellow-mittened hands into her coat pockets. "I made it clear to him I would be thrilled to work with him if our relationship is strictly professional. But honestly? I didn't like him, and I'm not sure I'd work with him even under the best of circumstances."

Anger surged through Quinn and he vowed right then and there he would make that man pay. Somehow. Some way.

But for now, he needed to focus on Sofia.

"Bastard." He wanted to pound the crap out of the guy. "Who the hell does he think he is?"

"A man who hasn't heard 'no' very often." She walked fast, giving away how angry the incident had made her. "An entitled, self-centered man who has let his reviews go to his head."

"I'm so sorry you had to deal with that. For what it's worth, it sounds like you handled it well."

"That reporter, Delaney, was lurking behind stage and overheard what happened." They crossed Central Park West and headed south to find entry onto a walking path. "At least if Fortier tries to discredit me or lie about what happened, I have a witness."

Hell. That hadn't even occurred to him. Sofia really could take care of herself and he respected the hell out of her for that.

"Would she tell the truth?" Quinn didn't know what to expect of the journalist who had seemed happy to sell anyone out for a story.

"To my surprise, I think she would." Sofia turned into the park ahead of him, still walking fast, as though demons followed close on her heels.

"Sofia." He took her arm gently, needing to get a better handle on what was happening here. "Please slow down. Should we go back there now and confront him? I'd be glad to—"

"No." She shifted her weight from one foot to the other, as if she had too much energy and didn't know where to put it all. "Definitely not. I'll call the ballet mistress tonight and tell her what happened. But I wasn't nervous. I was cool and professional. I danced the best I ever have. So, on some level, it was a good day because I drew on new strengths I didn't know I had." She stood still again, her wide blue eyes landing on his and seeming to really see him for the first time. "I'm only getting nervous again now because… you're here. And you said we needed to talk?"

Right. He'd asked for this audience, not realizing she'd just had one of the hardest days of her life. He tried reaching for her bag again.

"Please. Let me carry this for you."

She bit her full bottom lip for a moment, then passed him the bag. He felt like some medieval knight who'd just gotten his lady's favor tied to his sword.

They kept walking east, roughly following the same path as last time without ever discussing it.

"First, my IT connection put me in touch with the web site that posted—"

"I saw Olena, the matchmaker my father hired. She is just his old friend, by the way, and not a professional. That's probably why my father didn't tell you anything about her when the two of you spoke. I'm sure he didn't want to throw a friend under the bus. But she was the one who gave Cameron my contact details." She waved away the incident like it was no longer a concern. "She didn't understand the kind of site where she posted my photo. She meant well, but she knows I'm taking over my dating life. I will be choosing all future dating prospects."

The words punched a hole through his chest. He felt the sting of cold winter air right in the center of it as they walked down the slope near Tavern on the Green. This time, there was no talk of beauty surrounding them. No mischievous attempts to taste beauty on her tongue.

"About that." He willed all his persuasive powers to the fore. "I didn't sleep last night, thinking about what you said."

"That makes two of us." She wrapped her arms around herself.

He hadn't expected that hint of vulnerability from her after the way she'd ended things the night before.

"Sofia, I didn't mean to mislead you," he said, his boots crunching the frozen patches of snow. He'd dressed casually in boots and jeans today, taking the day off from work to focus on her. He'd take all damn month off if he needed to. "I understand how it might seem that way, but everything between us happened so fast. We went from planning how to stop a media storm to figuring out our dating history, and then getting to know each other for real in those phone calls—which I very much enjoyed—to trying to figure out where the matchmaking leak came from."

"I was focused on recovering from jet lag and impressing a lecherous ass." Her voice wound around him with a comfortable intimacy that he wished could last a lifetime.

She was that damn special to him.

"But we never lacked for conversation, did we?" he prodded, trying to justify his actions. "I didn't mention my grandfather's will at first because I didn't plan on following through. I planned to put his feet to the fire about the thing when he got back from China. Make him see reason. Marriage is too important to use as some bargaining chip in a business transaction."

Sofia glanced at him, giving him an assessing look through her lashes.

"If you really believe that—"

"I swear it. I sat up all night thinking about how I could convince you of it. I woke up my attorney and had her write up contracts to show you where I would renounce all rights to McNeill Resorts so you'd believe me." He opened his coat to show her a sheaf of crumpled papers. "I signed them, then discarded them an hour later, remembering how dismissive you sounded about using contracts in a personal relationship."

She nibbled a snowflake off her bottom lip. "Was I?"

"You suggested we should be able to arrange for dates without the help of a legally binding agreement." He withdrew the crumpled papers and handed them to her. "I'm only showing them to you now to illustrate how hard I tried to figure out how to convince you."

Heading east onto quieter pathways, they passed a horse-drawn carriage full of tourists snapping photos, but other than that there wasn't much traffic here.

"Convince me of what, exactly?" Sofia stopped near a field full of halfhearted snowmen, a few of which wore empty coffee cups for hats.

"I hadn't thought through what it meant to bring up marriage last night since I was wrecked after hearing about Gramps' condition." He reached for her free hand, pulling it from her pocket so he could hold it in both of his. "You haven't known me for long, so you couldn't know how unusual it is for me to talk without having any kind of agenda. But that is what has been so great about you. I got comfortable thinking we could talk about anything. But I had no business putting you in that kind of position."

"So you never meant to propose." She seemed to be tracking the conversation carefully, making him realize she was very much paying attention now.

Because she cared? Because she shared some of his feelings?

Fresh hope filled some of that hole in his chest and he took his time to get the words right for her.

"My brain was telling me to find any way possible to keep a ring on your finger so that that we could keep exploring whatever is happening between us. I sure didn't want to break off our fake engagement right when I realized I'm falling in love with you."

Sofia held a contract in her hand—signed by one of the country's wealthiest men—that stated in no uncertain terms he would relinquish all rights to his grandfather's legacy.

For her, he'd done that incredibly foolish thing.

That had floored her on a day when she thought she couldn't be any more surprised by life.

But then he told her he was falling for her and it was like what her mother had told her about beauty— you didn't see it. You experienced it all around you.

She stood inside one of those beautiful moments right now with a man so important to her she could no longer imagine life without him.

"I know it sounds crazy," he started.

She tucked the contract into his pocket and squeezed his hands tightly through her beautiful yellow mittens that made her happy.

The mittens that made her think she had inherited some of her mother's joyous outlook on life.

"It doesn't sound crazy. I was there, remember?" She echoed his words from the night before when she'd told him the sex was so good the first time she'd thought she dreamed it.

"I remember." His voice deepened as he stepped closer.

"I was falling in love, too," she admitted, her voice hoarse in a throat clogged with emotions.

"Was?" He stood toe-to-toe with her now. She had to look up at him.

"Am." She breathed the word between their lips as they stood together in the snowfall. "I am falling in love with you, Quinn. And I do see you for the man you are."

He kissed her, answering all her questions and easing all her doubts. Her heart swelled with new joy that crowded out everything else, making her wonder how she could have ever believed there was any other place for her in the world than at his side.

His arms wrapped around her, sheltering her. She breathed him in, his scent and touch already so familiar to her.

"I don't want to lose you, Sofia," he said between kisses. "Whatever it takes to convince you, to keep you, I will do it." He sealed his mouth to hers and only broke the kiss when an older lady rode past them on a bicycle, ringing her bell at them and giving them a thumbs-up.

Sofia laughed, feeling a ghost of her mother's happy spirit in that sweet, romantic gesture.

"You're not going to lose me." Her whole world felt new and full of possibilities, their lives as mingled as their puffy breaths merging in the cold air.

"Then it's the happiest day of my life so far. How should we celebrate?" he asked, tucking her under his arm to walk past the pond toward East Sixty-First where the Pierre waited.

His home.

"First, we're going to burn that contract." She patted the pocket where she'd shoved the papers. "Because I want you to support your grandfather's business and fulfill his legacy with your brothers."

"That's generous of you, but it sounds too tame for a celebration." Quinn dropped a kiss on top of her hair.

"Then we're going to make love all day," she whispered in his ear as they walked.

"I can't wait for that." The husky note in his voice assured her how much he meant it.

"Then we're going to come up with a plan to help me find a way to have a career after dance that doesn't involve Idris the Idiot."

"I hope it involves me punching him into next year." Quinn's jaw flexed.

"Probably not, but we'll leave it open for negotiation." Sofia let him lead her into the beautiful building where he lived, wondering if she'd ever get used to this kind of opulence.

"Can I make a suggestion?" Quinn asked, hitting the button for his private elevator.

"Of course." She bet he had a hot tub in that extravagant place of his. Her knees, at least, would get used to luxury in a hurry.

"I'd like to replace that monstrosity of a ring from my brother with something that looks more like you." He must have seen the surprise she felt because he rushed to explain. "Not that it's a proposal. We can take all the time you want to date. But as long as the world thinks we're engaged…"

"You weren't kidding about keeping a ring on my finger, were you?" She stepped into the elevator, grateful when the cabin doors shut behind them, sealing them in privacy.

"We don't have to comment on it, or issue any statements, or explain anything to anyone. We can just date and be mysterious about our plans." His blue eyes sparkled with a happiness she hadn't seen in them before. Also, a hint of sensual wickedness that she *had* seen before. And thoroughly enjoyed.

She had the feeling it was the same look in her eyes.

"Right. Because what we do is no one else's business. And we each have a partner we can trust." She felt dizzy from the rush of the elevator up to his floor.

The rush of love for a man who knew her better than any other.

A man who had spent all night thinking about how to show her he loved her.

When the elevator door opened and let them out into his apartment, Sofia fell into his arms, dragging him toward the first bed she found.

"I'm going to make you happy, Sofia." He kissed the words into her neck while she walked backward, peeling off her coat.

She smiled against his shoulder as she pushed off his jacket, too.

"You already have."

* * * * *

If you loved this story,
don't miss the next two installments in
THE MᴄNEILL MAGNATES:
THE MAGNATE'S MARRIAGE MERGER
(June 2017)
HIS ACCIDENTAL HEIR
(July 2017)
then
pick up these other sexy and emotional reads
from Joanne Rock!

HIS SECRETARY'S SURPRISE FIANCÉ
SECRET BABY SCANDAL

Available now from Harlequin Desire!

and

PROMISES UNDER THE PEACH TREE
NIGHTS UNDER THE TENNESSEE STARS
DANCES UNDER THE HARVEST MOON

Available now from Harlequin Superromance!

* * *

If you're on Twitter, tell us what you think
of Harlequin Desire! #harlequindesire

*Superstar Nate Tucker has no interest in the spoiled pop
princess determined to ensnare him, but when a secret
affair with her quiet sister, Mia, results in a baby on the
way, he'll do whatever it takes to claim Mia as his.*

Read on for a sneak peek at
LITTLE SECRET, RED HOT SCANDAL
by Cat Schield

Mia had made her choice and it hadn't been him.

"How've you been?" He searched her face for some
sign she'd suffered as he had, lingering over the circles
under her eyes and the downward turn to her mouth. To
his relief she didn't look happy, but that didn't stop her
from putting on a show.

"Things have been great."

"Tell me the truth." He was asking after her welfare,
but what he really wanted to know was if she'd missed
him.

"I'm great. Really."

"I hope your sister gave you a little time off."

"Ivy was invited to a charity event in South Beach and
we extended our stay a couple days to kick back and soak
up some sun."

Ivy demanded all Mia's time and energy. That Nate
had spent any alone time with Mia during Ivy's eight-
week stint on his tour was nothing short of amazing.

They'd snuck around like teenage kids. The danger of getting caught promoted intimacy. And at first, Nate found the subterfuge amusing. It got old fast.

It had bothered Nate that Ivy treated Mia like an employee instead of a sister. She never seemed to appreciate how Mia's kind and thoughtful behavior went above and beyond the role of personal assistant.

"I don't like the way we left things between us," Nate declared, taking a step in her direction.

Mia took a matching step backward. "You asked for something I couldn't give you."

"I asked for you to come to Las Vegas with me."

"We'd barely known each other two months." It was the same excuse she'd given him three weeks ago and it rang as hollow now as it had then. "And I couldn't leave Ivy."

"She could've found another assistant." He'd said the same thing the morning after the tour ended. The night after Mia had stayed with him until the sun crested the horizon.

"I'm not just her assistant. I'm her sister," Mia said, now as then. "She needs me."

I need you.

He wouldn't repeat the words. It wouldn't do any good. She'd still choose obligation to her sister over being happy with him.

And he couldn't figure out why.

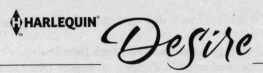

HARLEQUIN® Desire

AVAILABLE MAY 2017

TRIPLETS FOR THE TEXAN

BY *USA TODAY* BESTSELLING AUTHOR

JANICE MAYNARD,

PART OF THE SIZZLING
TEXAS CATTLEMAN'S CLUB: BLACKMAIL SERIES.

Wealthy Texas doctor Troy "Hutch" Hutchinson is the one who got away. Now he's back and ready to make things right, but Simone is already expecting three little surprises of her own...

AND DON'T MISS A SINGLE INSTALLMENT OF

TEXAS CATTLEMAN'S CLUB:

BLACKMAIL

No secret—or heart—is safe in Royal, Texas...

The Tycoon's Secret Child
by *USA TODAY* bestselling author Maureen Child

Two-Week Texas Seduction by Cat Schield

Reunited with the Rancher
by *USA TODAY* bestselling author Sara Orwig

Expecting the Billionaire's Baby by Andrea Laurence

Triplets for the Texan
by *USA TODAY* bestselling author Janice Maynard

AND

June 2017: *A Texas-Sized Secret* by *USA TODAY* bestselling author Maureen Child
July 2017: *Lone Star Baby Scandal* by Golden Heart® Award winner Lauren Canan
August 2017: *Tempted by the Wrong Twin* by *USA TODAY* bestselling author Rachel Bailey
September 2017: *Taking Home the Tycoon* by *USA TODAY* bestselling author Catherine Mann
October 2017: *Billionaire's Baby Bind* by *USA TODAY* bestselling author Katherine Garbera
November 2017: *The Texan Takes a Wife* by *USA TODAY* bestselling author Charlene Sands
December 2017: *Best Man Under the Mistletoe* by *USA TODAY* bestselling author Kathie DeNosky

Whatever You're Into… Passionate Reads

Looking for more passionate reads from Harlequin®?
Fear not! Harlequin® Presents, Harlequin® Desire and
Harlequin® Blaze offer you irresistible romance stories
featuring powerful heroes.

◈HARLEQUIN *Presents*®

Do you want alpha males, decadent glamour and jet-set
lifestyles? Step into the sensational, sophisticated world of
Harlequin® Presents, where sinfully tempting heroes ignite a
fierce and wickedly irresistible passion!

◈HARLEQUIN *Desire*

Harlequin® Desire novels are powerful, passionate and
provocative contemporary romances set against a backdrop of
wealth, privilege and sweeping family saga. Alpha heroes with
a soft side meet strong-willed but vulnerable heroines amid a
dramatic world of divided loyalties, high-stakes conflict and
intense emotion.

◈HARLEQUIN *Blaze*

Harlequin® Blaze stories sizzle with strong heroines and
irresistible heroes playing the game of modern love and lust.
They're fun, sexy and always steamy.

Be sure to check out our full selection of books
within each series every month!

www.Harlequin.com

HPASSION2016

HARLEQUIN®
A *Romance* FOR EVERY MOOD™

Love the Harlequin book you just read?

Your opinion matters.

Review this book on your favorite book site, review site, blog or your own social media properties and share your opinion with other readers!

Be sure to connect with us at:
Harlequin.com/Newsletters
Facebook.com/HarlequinBooks
Twitter.com/HarlequinBooks

Get 2 Free Books,

Plus 2 Free Gifts—

just for trying the Reader Service!